Rocambole

also by Frank J. Morlock

Sherlock Holmes: The Grand Horizontals

Arsène Lupin vs. Sherlock Holmes: The Stage Play
(*adapted from the play by Victor Darlay & Henry de Gorsse*)

Frankenstein Meets the Hunchback of Notre-Dame
(*adapted from the plays by
Charles Nodier,
Antoine Nicolas Béraud & Jean Toussaint Merle
and
Victor Hugo, Paul Foucher & Paul Meurice*)

Lord Ruthven the Vampire
(*adapted from the plays by
Charles Nodier and Eugène Scribe*)

The Return of Lord Ruthven
(*adapted from the play by Alexandre Dumas*)

by
Auguste Anicet-Bourgeois
and
Lucien Dabril

based on the novels by
Pierre-Alexis Ponson du Terrail

translated and adapted by
Frank J. Morlock

A Black Coat Press Book

Acknowledgements: We are indebted to Dagny for typing the plays and David McDonnell for proofreading the typescript.

To Robert Haas for many years of friendship.

FJM

Visit our website at www.blackcoatpress.com

Table of Contents

BIBLIOTHÈQUE
MARABOUT
géant
PONSON DU TERRAIL
ROCAMBOLE
1
L'HÉRITAGE MYSTÉRIEUX

Introduction

It is almost impossible to discuss 19th-century French *romans feuilletons*–thus named because they were serialized in the pages of daily newspapers–without mentioning the name of Pierre-Alexis Ponson du Terrail (1829-1871), the author of the saga of *Rocambole*, a sprawling series of nine novels published between 1857 and 1870.

The "Righter of Wrongs" was one of the most important characters to emerge in popular fiction and melodrama at that time. Rocambole began his career on the wrong side of the law, as a young adventurer who was the right-hand man of master villain Andrea de Felipone, a.k.a. Sir Williams; but, like his literary descendants, Raffles, Arsène Lupin and the Saint, he soon switched sides and became a hero, challenging and, ultimately, defeating his former master, and many more colorful villains thereafter.

As was later the case with Sherlock Holmes, The Shadow and Doc Savage, Rocambole eventually gathered around him a group of dedicated assistants with colorful names, selected from various slices of society, ready to drop everything to help their master. He often operated in the shadows, pulling strings from behind the scenes, sometimes appearing as the mysterious "Man in Grey," hiding his penetrating gaze behind blue-tinted spectacles.[1] Rocambole also mastered the skills of the Orient and inherited the secrets of ancient Tibetan and other equally exotic civilizations. In short, Rocambole became more than a mere man, he was the first modern, literary superhero, a kind of Byronic superman blended with a Parisian street urchin.

Ponson du Terrail's early works squarely belonged to the Gothic-styled *roman noir*: His novel *La Baronne Trépassée* [*The Late Baroness*] (1852) was a murky, Ann Radcliffe-like tale of revenge in the macabre surroundings of the 1700s Black Forest. When, in 1857, he embarked on writing the first novel of the *Rocambole* saga, *L'Héritage Mystérieux* [*The Mysterious Inheritance*], for the daily newspaper *La Patrie*, he merely meant to copy the successes of Eugène Sue's earlier bestseller, *Les Mystères de Paris* [*The Mysteries of Paris*] (1842-43),[2] and of Paul Féval's *Les Mystères de Londres* [*The Mysteries of London*] (1843-44).[3] Prince Rodolphe became Armand de Kergaz, La Chouette, Maman Fipart, and Tortillard, Rocambole. But then. something truly unexpected happened...

---

[1] A gimmick Arsène Lupin will reuse as "Jim Barnett" in *L'Agence Barnett & Cie.*

[2] The morality of Ponson du Terrail's novels is far more simplistic than that of Sue and Féval, and he never challenges the existing social order. However, it is worth noting that, if Sir Williams is pure evil, its two opponents, Rocambole and Baccarat, a reformed prostitute, are far more "grey" than black or white.

[3] forthcoming from Black Coat Press. The London-based *Gentlemen of the night* mentioned on p. 228 are indeed the same crime ring introduced by Féval in *Les Mystères de Londres.*

That resourceful boy, Rocambole, an orphan, whose origins are unknown, the adopted son of the horrible old crone Maman Fipart, began to take over the narrative!

When we first met Rocambole in the novel, Ponson du Terrail had made him 14. But as the character became the nefarious Sir Williams' protégé, he showed so much potential, displayed so much charisma–and was so popular with readers!–that Ponson, quickly sensing that he was on to a good thing, aged him in the course of a few chapters, and Rocambole suddenly turned 16! The rest, as they say, is history.

The continuing saga of *Rocambole* became a huge success, providing a constant and considerable source of revenue to Ponson du Terrail, who continued churning out his colorful rogue's adventures.[*]

Ponson du Terrail, like no one before him, understood the art of the serial form of publication in its own right, and in particular the cliffhanger and the famous phrase "*à suivre au prochain numéro*" [to be continued in our next issue]. *Rocambole* was created out of real collaboration between the author and his public. Like Sir Arthur Conan Doyle, Ponson du Terrail almost got rid of his creation when he horribly mutilated Rocambole and dispatched him to the forced labor camp of Toulon at the end of *Les Exploits de Rocambole*, then revived him in response to public outcry.

In August 1870, as Ponson du Terrail had just embarked on a new serial entitled *La Corde du Pendu* [*The Hanged Man's Rope*], Emperor Napoléon III

---

[4] For more information about Rocambole, the character is the subject of a chapter in our book *Shadowmen: Heroes and Villains of French Pulp Fiction*, Black Coat Press, 2003 (ISBN 0-9740711-3-7).

surrendered to Germany. Ponson was forced to flee Paris; on January 20, 1871, he died prematurely at age 42, sadly leaving the saga of *Rocambole* uncompleted.

Rocambole's importance in the history of French popular fiction cannot be underestimated. It represents the transition from the old-fashioned Gothic novel to modern heroic fiction, in the sense that it created and virtually defined all the archetypes of modern superheroes and supervillains. The fact that the word *rocambolesque* has become common in French to label any kind of fantastic adventure, is the best testament of which Ponson du Terrail could have dreamed.

The first of the two plays gathered in this volume is a perfect example of the then-popular tradition of quickly and routinely adapting bestsellers from the literary medium into stage plays, as we do today by turning them into films or television series.

To quote John McCormick,[5] "What gave *Rocambole* his appeal in the *feuilleton* clearly was absent when transferred to the stage, though his more general influence on end-of-the-century melodrama should not be underestimated. The novels were a good example of work drawing on melodrama for inspiration, and, in turn, helping broaden the repertoire of melodrama with the notion of a gentleman-criminal operating his own system of social justice with a sort of tacit license to do so (rather like a court fool). The *feuilleton* had taken over completely from the theater as the mass medium, and it was no longer a question of reaching a wider public by adapting a novel for the stage."

---

[5] *Popular Theatres of Nineteenth Century France*, Routledge, London and New York (1993).

Auguste Anicet-Bourgeois' (1806-1871) adaptation of *Rocambole* [6] was first staged at the popular Théâtre de l'Ambigu in 1864. Interestingly, this was a mere three years after Ponson du Terrail had "buried" his character in the forced labor camp of Toulon in *Les Exploits de Rocambole*, and a year before he triumphantly brought him back in *La Résurrection de Rocambole*.

Two years prior, Anicet-Bourgeois had adapted Paul Féval's swashbuckling classic *Le Bossu* [*The Hunchback*] and was, therefore, an ideal choice for *Rocambole*. His version drew mainly from the second and third novels in the series: *Le Club des Valets de Coeurs* [*The Club of the Jack of Hearts*] and *Les Exploits de Rocambole* [*The Exploits of Rocambole*]. It moves briskly, without bothering the audience with too much exposition, reasonably assuming a certain familiarity with the characters. It is, to paraphrase William Goldman, the "best bits" from the books.

To put things in perspective, and using the 1960s Marabout edition as a common yardstick, Paul Féval's *The Black Coats: 'Salem Street* [7] clocks in at 414 pages. *The Mysterious Inheritance*, by comparison, is a hefty 532 pages, *The Club of the Jack of Hearts* a mammoth 796 pages and *The Exploits of Rocambole* a truly gargantuan 1076 pages!

In Anicet-Bourgeois' play, Rocambole meets Andrea, a.k.a. Sir Williams, much later in the villain's career. His duel with his half-brother Armand de Kergaz is not mentioned and the infamous Club of the Jack of Hearts is already in the past, relegated to mere

---

[6] Some bibliographies credit playwright Ernest Blum as having worked uncredited on that adaptation.

[7] Published by Black Coat Press (ISBN 1-932983-46-5).

background information. The plot to steal the Chamery inheritance and the Sallandrera fortune is taken straight from *The Exploits of Rocambole*. But in Ponson du Terrail's novel, by then, Rocambole is no longer Sir Williams' youthful apprentice, as he was in *The Club of the Jack of Hearts*, but has already become the Master. And his ultimate defeat at Baccarat's hands is far more tragic than the fate arranged for him by Anicet-Bourgeois.

Combining, as it were, the relationships between the characters of *The Club of the Jack of Hearts*, and the plot of *The Exploits of Rocambole*, Anicet-Bourgeois has also tinkered somewhat with the characters. For unfathomable reasons, Baccarat, whose real name is Louise Charmet, is no longer Cerise's older sister, the latter being now a "Mademoiselle Bertin." As for Maman Fipart, the repulsive old crone from the novel has turned into a dotty old aunt. Well, Hollywood has done worse!

Les Aventures de Rocambole by Lucien Dabril, on the other hand, is a more modern adaptation, written in 1951, reportedly because Dabril's mother was a fan of the character; no doubt, the woman had been enthralled by the popular 1947 feature film adaptation by Jacques de Baroncelli that had cast the handsome Pierre Brasseur as Rocambole, the beautiful Sophie Desmarets as Baccarat and Lucien Nat as the machiavellian Sir Williams. The play was originally staged and directed by Roger Planchon (himself a dramatist), but does not seem to have left much of a mark otherwise. It was soon eclipsed by the far more popular television series of 1964 that starred Pierre Vernier as Rocambole, Marianne

Girard as Baccarat and the prodigious Jean Topart as Sir Williams.

Dabril's adaptation limits itself to using story elements taken from *L'Héritage Mystérieux* and is more faithful to Ponson du Terrail's than was Anicet-Bourgeois'. It is a good primer on the origins of Rocambole. Of course, in the original novel, Sir Williams doesn't die but just goes on to found the Club of the Jack of Hearts and commit more villainy in the eponymous second novel.

In both plays, Rocambole shows promise, but hasn't yet become the full-fledged hero of Ponson du Terrail's later novel. He is still ambiguously caught between good and evil, and his redemption in Anicet-Bourgeois' play is but a pale shadow of his prodigious ordeal in *La Résurrection de Rocambole*. At the end of that novel, Baccarat sees Rocambole deliberately let the woman whom he dearly loves marry another, worthier suitor; then and only then, she knows that Rocambole has finally exorcised the ghost of his evil mentor Sir Williams, and she whispers in his ear a single word: "Redemption!"

Jean-Marc Lofficier

Rocambole

by

Auguste Anicet-Bourgeois

Characters

Joseph Fipart, a.k.a. Rocambole, Major Avatar
Andrea de Felipone, a.k.a. Sir Williams, Dr. Gordon
Louise Charmet, a.k.a. Baccarat

and in order of appearance:
Gertrude
Venture
Maman Fipart
Jean Guignon
The Marquis de Chamery
Cerise Bertin
Tulipe Hubert
Albert de Chamery
Alphonse
Fanny
Baptiste
The Boatmen and Boatgirls of Croissy
Tomas
Concepcion de Sallandrera
The Duke de Sallandrera
Antoine

The action takes place in 1858 in Paris and the surrounding area.

PROLOGUE

The Club of the Jack of Hearts

A room serving as a library, opening in the back on another room. To the left, there a door leading to the Marquis de Chamery's room. To the right, facing the door, there is a window opening on a balcony. At the back, part of the library is at the left and, on the right, there is an iron safe set into the wall. In a corner there is a table covered with papers forming a work desk. Near this table there is an armchair of the type used by convalescents. The room, the hangings, the furniture all very stern-looking. A candelabra with two candles is on the table; it is the only source of light in the library.

AT RISE, Gertrude enters from the back, as if she had just escorted someone out. Venture, dressed in a modest livery and affecting an attraction more modest still, is finishing lighting the candles.

GERTRUDE: There, the doctor's gone.
VENTURE: Well done, Gertrude. What did he say?
GERTRUDE: That he found Monsieur de Chamery very ill.
VENTURE: Then, it's bad luck for me. The Marquis will give you a settlement. You've worked for him more than 26 years, whereas I, who only came here six months ago, will have to seek other employment.

(Gertrude sits in the armchair and unwinds a roll of wool which she makes Venture hold while she rewinds it.)

GERTRUDE: Poor man! Hold my wool, will you?

VENTURE: With pleasure.

GERTRUDE: If you must leave us I will miss you, Venture.

VENTURE: That will be a great honor you'll be doing me.

GERTRUDE: You are pleasant and much more clever than that imbecile of a Dominique who left us without saying why he was going. Would you believe that he, a man, was more afraid than I? In this old hotel, Rue de l'Ouest! The Marquis came to live here three months ago and...

VENTURE: What! He was afraid? A strong, ruddy-faced fellow like that?

GERTRUDE: Ah, but he became all pale when they whispered in front of him of the Jack of Hearts!

VENTURE: Oh! That's a good one! He was afraid of a playing card?

GERTRUDE: You don't know what the Jack of Hearts are, do you?

VENTURE: Excuse me, but I am very well versed in the games of *piquet* and *bezigue*.

GERTRUDE: Fool! I am speaking to you of a gang of thieves, who are unfortunately very well-known around the Capital.

VENTURE: My, my...

GERTRUDE: And these rogues do not hesitate to kill to steal!

VENTURE: Ah, that's nasty! But why do they call themselves the Jack of Hearts?

GERTRUDE: Because they always leave that card as their calling card everywhere they've been—inside the safes they've emptied—on the bleeding wound of a man they've just murdered—always a jack of hearts!

VENTURE: That's funny. No, I mean that's horrible. But it sounds quite fanciful. Do you really believe in this tale?

GERTRUDE: Yes, I do!

(*A loud ringing is heard. Gertrude lets out a cry and lets her wool fall.*)

GERTRUDE: Ah! What's that?

VENTURE (*picking up the ball*): That? Unless I'm mistaken, that's Monsieur ringing

GERTRUDE: Yes, yes, and he's ringing for me. If I need you, I'll call you. How stupid! I am all atremble!

(*Gertrude leaves.*)

VENTURE (*watching her go*): There's a nice old woman who would faint if I told her "I am one of the most active members of the Club of the Jack of Hearts. I've been sent here by Andrea de Felipone, our leader. I know the Marquis de Chamery's illness better than his Doctor, and I know that it can't be cured. The Marquis has written to his Notary regarding his will. I've taken that letter to my master and now await his orders."

(*Gertrude returns.*)

GERTRUDE: The Marquis is growing impatient because his Notary hasn't come yet. He wants someone to go and fetch him—Maître Aubernon, Rue du Louvre.

VENTURE: Of course. I will go at once. (*aside*) But I won't bring him back.

GERTRUDE: No, not you. The Marquis wants you to stay here. He asked me to send Little Jean instead.

VENTURE: Who?

GERTRUDE: The errand boy outside. (*she goes to the window and looks into the street.*) Great! He's not at his usual place!

VENTURE: Then the Marquis will have to wait... (*a different ringing*) Good Lord–a visitor!

GERTRUDE: Perhaps it's Maître Aubernon?

VENTURE (*aside*): That would greatly surprise me.

GERTRUDE: Heavens! It's Maman Fipart, our seamstress. Come in, Maman Fipart, come in! I expected you yesterday.

(*Maman Fipart, an old crone, enters.*)

MAMAN FIPART: True, true, I'm a bit late, but what a state your linen was in! We worked hard, Cerise and I, to fix it.

VENTURE: Cerise?

MAMAN FIPART: My niece, my only consolation in my old age! Without her, I don't know what would become of me. Without her, I couldn't work. My eyes aren't what they used to be. Too many tears!

GERTRUDE: Yes, I know. You lost your husband four years ago. He was a good man.

MAMAN FIPART: Ah, Madame Gertrude! He was the very incarnation of honor and honesty–and a hard worker, too! A model artisan, he was. He earned good wages, we had savings, we were happy. God took him from me.

GERTRUDE: But you still have a son. Although I've heard...

MAMAN FIPART: What?

GERTRUDE (*embarrassed*): Well, that he's been kicked from many a job, and that if he desires something of yours, it's as good as stolen.

MAMAN FIPART: No, Madame Gertrude, don't call my son a thief. 'Tis true that he took some money from us, but my God, that money was his, too! If my husband had lived, Joseph might have turned out better. Perhaps it's my fault. Then, you know, they always make things worse than they are. Joseph was lazy and that's been his misfortune. He likes to have fun and he's made some bad acquaintances. But inside, he was ashamed. He didn't tell these villains his real name, no, he didn't! To them, he was known only as "Rocambole." And these men dragged him down no further than he wished. The memory of his father has always protected him from committing the worst crimes... I gave him a talisman!

VENTURE AND GERTRUDE: A talisman?

MAMAN FIPART: One day—a beautiful day, that was—the master of the workshop where my husband worked gave him a silver medallion, to honor him as the best and more honest of all his workers. My husband always wore it on a chain around his neck, with a lock of my hair—it was his badge of honor! After he died, I took that medallion and gave it to Joseph, and made him swear to always wear it as his father had done, in his memory and as an example.

VENTURE: I bet the scamp pawned it, right?

MAMAN FIPART: No, sir, he kept it, but—

GERTRUDE: —But ignored its meaning. You're a good woman, Madame Fipart. Whatever happens, I will always send you my business. Here's your money. It's late and it's far to Belleville–that's where you live, no?

MAMAN FIPART: Yes, Rue des Moulins, No. 27, the house of Mademoiselle Tulipe Hubert.

VENTURE: Tulipe?

MAMAN FIPART: Yes, she's my landlady. Goodbye, Madame Gertrude! Monsieur Venture! 'Til another time.

(*She leaves.*)

GERTRUDE: Now, there's a *good* woman.

VENTURE: With a "promising" son. A name like that! Rocambole! It speaks volumes!

GERTRUDE: It's not for us to judge. (*going to window*) Ah! The errand boy is back at his post. (*shouting*) Hey, little fella! Come up, come up quick! We've got need of your services!

VENTURE (*who has been looking*): I don't know that lad.

GERTRUDE: He was sick for the last two months and didn't return until today. Let me open the door for him.

(*She opens the door. Jean Guignon enters. He is dressed as an errand boy. He has a good and honest face and a naïve expression.*)

JEAN GUIGNON (*to Gertrude*): I'm well enough to serve you today, Madame Gertrude, and your master, too. I got out of the hospital this morning and I haven't had any work yet.

GERTRUDE: Good. You'll take a letter that is still being written to.... By the way, what did happen to you? The last time I saw you down there, you didn't seem sick at all. Did a roof tile fall on your head?

JEAN GUIGNON: No. A man fell on my arms.

VENTURE: A man?

JEAN GUIGNON: You may find that surprising, Monsieur, but me, when I get up in the morning, I always ask myself what catastrophe is going to happen to me that day. You see, when I was little, my friends nicknamed me Jean "Guignon," which means "bad luck," because I really had bad luck! First, I'm my mother's tenth child. I was born on Friday the 13th in the first quarter of an April moon. Those are evil portents. I soured the milk of five nurses, three from Burgundy, one from Picardy and a goat. When the Draft was reinstated, I drew No. 1. I had a girl friend who swore she'd wait for me. Finally, after four years, a minor injury got me out of the Army. So I went home, all the while telling myself, "Sweetums–that was my girlfriend–Sweetums' gonna be real happy 'cuz I'm home three years early." But what do you think happened when I got back to my village? The bells were ringing. The whole village was at the church. I rushed there and what do you think I saw?

VENTURE: Sweetums getting married?

JEAN GUIGNON: No. Sweetums baptizing her third child! Then, from despair, I rushed to Paris and took the job of errand boy. Here, I made all new acquaintances. My luck seemed to change; I met a good girl, a hard worker, pretty and fresh like her name–Cerise. That's a sweet name, isn't it? I'd like to marry her, so I went down to her place to ask for her hand. As I was passing through the Rue de Varennes, I saw a crowd looking up at a man beating capers on his balcony. It gave you gooseflesh just to look at him up there! He was, perhaps, a student of Leotard. Finally, he tried a last pirouette, but this time, his head twisted and he missed his footing.

Everybody recoiled. Like an idiot, I extended my arms forward! And he fell on me straight from the third floor.

GERTRUDE: The poor man!

JEAN GUIGNON: No, poor me!

GERTRUDE: Why? Didn't he kill himself?

JEAN GUIGNON: No! He dislocated my shoulder, that's what he did.

(*Ringing from the left.*)

GERTRUDE: Ah! Monsieur has finished writing his letter. Come take it, then leave by the service stairs.

(*Gertrude leads Jean to the Marquis' room, unwittingly placing her hand on his shoulder.*)

JEAN GUIGNON: Ouch!

GERTRUDE: What's wrong?

JEAN GUIGNON (*rubbing his shoulder*): Just a souvenir from Leotard's student.

(*They go into the Marquis' room.*)

VENTURE: Uh-oh. Maître Aubernon mustn't be informed. He mustn't come. Oh, my word, too bad for that poor Guignon, but he can't be allowed to go to the Notary's. A flower pot is less heavy than a man–I'd rather not kill this poor devil, but I must stop him. (*looking at the window*) There he comes.

(*Venture grabs a flower pot and drops it.*)

JEAN GUIGNON (*outside*): Ouch! Oh my head! My head! (*sound of a collapse*)

VENTURE (*still looking*): They're picking him up... taking him to the wine seller's. He doesn't seem too badly injured–that makes me feel better–and he won't do his errand. We won't see Maître Aubernon.

GERTRUDE (*entering from the back*): Come in, sir, come in.

VENTURE (*turning*): Huh?

(*Gertrude enters with a man dressed in black with a white tie and white frill, grey wig and bluish glasses. He has a respectable air.*)

GERTRUDE: Someone's just left to fetch you.

VENTURE (*aside*): Who was it who told him to come?

GERTRUDE: I'll announce you to Monsieur le Marquis.

VENTURE: Excuse me, Monsieur. Are you Maître Aubernon, the Notary?

ANDREA (*for it is he*): No, my friend, I'm one of his clerks and it's he who has sent me with this letter for the Marquis de Chamery. (*He hands a letter to Gertrude.*)

VENTURE: Shouldn't you tell us–

ANDREA: My name? Of course. Forgive me. Nothing could be more proper. Here's my card. (*He hands a card to Venture–a playing card!*)

VENTURE (*aside*): A jack of hearts!

ANDREA (*low*): Imbecile.

VENTURE (*low*): The master!

GERTRUDE: Well?

VENTURE: Oh, go ahead, announce him. The gentleman is a proper Notary.

ANDREA: Go, my good woman, go.

(*Exit Gertrude. Andrea takes off his glasses and goes to sit in an armchair.*)

VENTURE: I can see how you are able to deceive just about anyone, seeing how you just fooled me, your oldest–associate.

ANDREA: You flatter me, my poor lad, you flatter me greatly. Let's get down to business. I've learned, through my network of spies in the provinces, that a Marquis de Chamery, old and without family, had just sold his vast estate in Brittany, and that, after having collected the sale price, had come to live alone in this modest house, accompanied only by his trusted governess and a servant. This Marquis is a miser who hoards a treasure that I fancy to possess. First, it was necessary to place someone on the inside. The governess was too loyal and the servant a nincompoop who could not be trusted. So I arranged to scare him away, and you were put in his place. That was six weeks ago...

VENTURE: God knows if, during that time, I haven't listened at the doors, spied on the old man and tried to wrest confidences from the old woman.

ANDREA: And yet, you still haven't figured out where the money is?

VENTURE: Well, there's a safe in here. I've seen rolls of gold coins inside, that I haven't touched of course. The real treasure is hidden elsewhere, but I've searched the house from top to bottom and...

ANDREA: ...And you haven't found a thing. You no longer even try. Still, you did find something of importance. A week ago, the Marquis received a letter... An important letter...

VENTURE: Yes! It almost transformed him. Now, he speaks of leaving Paris, of traveling–

ANDREA: That's why I decided to rush our business. Thanks to your skills with poison, the Marquis is now gravely ill; so, he naturally wants to put his affairs in order and wrote to Maître Aubernon, his Notary, to notify him that he wishes to draw up a new will... It was very easy for me to take the place of the Notary and I've come here to receive that will that will finally tell us where he's hidden his millions.

VENTURE: Here's the Marquis.

(The Marquis enters, supported by Gertrude. He is old and frail, but broken more by sorrow than by age. He's dressed in a long white robe, over white pajamas and slippers. Andrea and Venture stand up and bow.)

VENTURE *(low to Andrea)*: You see that the dose was very well measured.

(With a gesture, the Marquis sends away Gertrude and Venture, and lets himself fall into an armchair while inviting the phony Notary to take a seat.)

MARQUIS DE CHAMERY: I am a stranger to Paris, Monsieur. I used Maître Aubernon's services purely because his office is near this house.

ANDREA: Maître Aubernon is himself very ill and begged me to—

MARQUIS DE CHAMERY: I understand, Monsieur. Your official function is a guarantee of honorability. I will tell you the secret I wanted to confide to your employer. Please sit down, Monsieur, nearer to me— closer—for my voice is growing tired. My strength is going and I have a long story to tell you.

ANDREA: I am listening, Monsieur le Marquis.

MARQUIS DE CHAMERY: Very well. I was once married to a woman much younger than I. The Marquise was a beautiful lady. I was very jealous, and yet during the first three years of our marriage, she gave me no reason to feel that way, not even the most innocent flirtation, never once besmirching the name she now bore. But then, a diplomatic mission from Spain brought one of her distant relatives–a Monsieur de Sallandrera.

ANDREA: Would you be speaking of the Duke de Sallandrera, who was for a long time the Spanish Ambassador to Brazil?

MARQUIS DE CHAMERY: The same. It was precisely to go to Rio de Janeiro that he left us. The Duke was still a young man. He couldn't see his charming cousin without falling in love with her. I soon had written proof of their love–their affair! When the Marquise later gave birth to a son, I suspected at once that the child was but the fruit of adultery and I swore that the bastard would neither inherit my fortune nor my name. But I was fearful of scandal. So I insisted that the child, entrusted to a nurse named Marianne, be raised far from my chateau. When he reached his third year, the Marquise begged me to return her son to her but I hesitated. I wanted to punish the mother–but I also pitied the child. Still, I was forced to make a decision. One night, a fire devoured Marianne's house. The next day, the firemen searched in vain throughout the ashes for the remains of the woman and child who surely had perished in that fire.

ANDREA: A fire lit by your orders?

MARQUIS DE CHAMERY: Yes.

ANDREA: So, you had condemned an innocent woman and child to death?

MARQUIS DE CHAMERY: You are mistaken, Monsieur. I didn't want the bastard to die, merely to disappear. That very night, Marianne, whom I had bribed, embarked on a ship with the child. Later, she resettled in Ireland in a little farm purchased with my money.

ANDREA: The firemen must have been surprised to not to find any evidence of bodies–

MARQUIS DE CHAMERY: Indeed, but no one doubted their deaths. My wife wept for 23 years for her son. Poor woman. (*stops and starts crying*)

ANDREA: What's wrong, Monsieur?

MARQUIS DE CHAMERY (*getting hold of himself*): Nothing. I'll continue. After the death of the Marquise, I resolved to change my life. I sold everything I owned. Thus, I realized a considerable sum of money...

ANDREA: Which you have kept in your home? That's extremely careless.

MARQUIS DE CHAMERY: In Brittany, I had no fear of thieves. Here, I have deposited it at the Banque de France.

ANDREA (*aside*): Ah! The Devil! It will be difficult to get it out of there. (*aloud*) And to whom do you wish to will this fortune?

MARQUIS DE CHAMERY: To the child–to my son.

ANDREA: Ah! I'm afraid, I no longer understand...

MARQUIS DE CHAMERY: Let me explain. Eight days ago, I received a letter from the Duke de Sallandrera. This letter informed me that Marianne, the nurse, tortured with remorse, had confessed to him that, following my instructions, she had set fire to her house and, later, used the pension I paid her to resettle in Ireland. There, she had raised young Albert–that's his name–who became handsome just like his mother. Faithful to my orders, she kept him ignorant of the name of his father. Albert applied himself to the arts, especially painting. Lately, he began to travel. His last letter to Marianne was posted from Madras. The poor woman didn't want to take his secret to her grave so she confessed to the Duke, whom she knew was a relative. She also sent him a few of my letters which she had kept. The Duke understood all too well my motives. Appraised of the situation for the first time, he decided to give me proof–irrefutable proof–of the Marquise's innocence and thus of Albert's legitimate birth. "When the young man returns to France," he wrote me, "let you, his true father, give him back his name and his fortune and I, Duke de Sallandrera, swear on my honor as a Grandee of Spain and on my faith as a Christian, to give Albert, Marquis of Chamery, my daughter, Concepcion de Sallandrera, to be his wife." I could no longer doubt his words. I wanted to leave, to find this son I had cast out–but ill as I am, I no longer have the time. So, in this holographic last will and testament, I have written out what I just confessed to you. I hereby recognize that Albert, the child raised by Marianne, is indeed my son. My only son! I will never see him. I won't be able to say to him: "Forgive me for all the wrongs I've done to you; forgive me for all the wrongs I did to your mother."

ANDREA: I see. So you would like me to safekeep the will and these accompanying letters?

MARQUIS DE CHAMERY: Not quite. I will place them under lock in this safe, built into this wall, the key of which never leaves my person. When I am no more, you will know where to find the will and you will undertake to execute it.

(*The Marquis rises, goes to open the safe and places the will and documents inside. Then, he hides the key in his pajamas. Feeling suddenly weak, he leans against the wall.*)

MARQUIS DE CHAMERY: There is a fortune of five millions there for my son, Monsieur.

ANDREA (*aside*): Five millions!

MARQUIS DE CHAMERY: I feel weak suddenly. Would you ring the bell?

(*Andrea rings. Gertrude and Venture appear.*)

GERTRUDE: Ah! My God! Monsieur, are you feeling ill?

MARQUIS DE CHAMERY: Yes, I can no longer get to my room alone. (*to Andrea*) Goodbye, Monsieur. If I never see you again–remember–remember!

(*The Marquis waves a weak goodbye to Andrea and returns to his room supported by Gertrude and Venture.*)

ANDREA (*alone*): Hmm. Stealing the money is impossible. One can't easily deceive the Banque de France. The Marquis' millions will only leave its vaults to pass into the hands of his Heir... Hmm. This suggests another tack... Whosoever possesses the will and is its beneficiary will eventually become the sole owner of the Chamery gold... I'd wage that a poor, starving artist, presently without name or fortune, won't refuse to share the millions that I, alone, can give him.

(*Venture emerges from the Marquis' room.*)

VENTURE: The Marquis is dying. He didn't even feel my hand when I slid it into his robe and pinched the key.

ANDREA: The governess?

VENTURE: She ran off like a madwoman to fetch the doctor.

ANDREA: The entire Faculty of Medicine of Paris couldn't save the life of a man whom I have condemned to death. His hour has come. Give me the key and keep an eye on what's going on.

(*Venture runs to the back to make sure no one comes from outside. Andrea takes the key and attempts to open the safe.*)

(*At this moment, the Marquis enters through the doorway on the left. He is pale, weak, more a ghost than a man. He sees Andrea turn the key in the lock of the safe. He drags himself, or rather hurls himself, forward and, in a supreme effort of will, grabs Andrea.*)

MARQUIS DE CHAMERY: Ah! Infamy!

(*Upon seeing the Marquis, Venture recoils in shocked. Even Andrea appears momentarily troubled. Suddenly, the wind blows out the candles. Andrea has regained his calm. With Venture's help, he takes the old man, now barely conscious, back to his room.*)

(*The stage remains empty and dark for a moment. Then we see an arm come in through the half-opened window on the right and raises the latch. A young man, rattily dressed, opens the window and stealthily jumps into the room. It is Rocambole.*)

ROCAMBOLE: An open window, that is to say: an invitation. Nothing but a small balcony to scale. No lights. No one in the street. No sounds from the house. How could one resist the temptation? A sick, old man, an old woman, a single servant–and a hidden treasure.

That's what I heard on the street. So I said to myself: Rocambole, my boy, there's an opportunity here. You can't go back to Maman Fipart. You sleep either on hot coals or icy-cold cobbles, and your wardrobe is dismal. That's no life for one with your talents. So the notion of snatching a pretty stash and beating it to another country and starting over becomes very appealing–and I think I might just be able to do it here. But first, let there be light! (*lights a match*) Now I can look around. (*he does*) Heavens, what do I see but a safe with the key still in its lock! The gods are smiling on me!

(*Rocambole goes to the sage, opens it and starts rifling through its contents. Suddenly, Andrea emerges from the Marquis' room. Upon seeing Rocambole, he stops.*)

ANDREA: By the Devil! Who's this man? Where did he come from?

(*Andrea pulls a dagger from his pocket and hurls himself at Rocambole. The young man, surprised, tries to resist but Andrea has the advantage. The older man soon has Rocambole trapped under his knees and is about to stab him when Venture appears, holding a candle. The light lights up the face of Rocambole. Andrea's arm remains suspended in mid-air.*)

ROCAMBOLE: Trapped! Ah, you've got a good grip–word of Rocambole.
VENTURE: Rocambole! (*stopping Andrea's arm*) One moment, master! I know who he is....

CURTAIN

ACT I

Scene I

A small garden in the back of a house in Belleville. To the right, there is a building composed of a ground floor and a first floor. To the left, another building, but this one advancing onto the stage so that the interior of the ground floor can be seen through an open window. There are garden chairs with their backs leaning against the wall on the left. To the rear, there is a small wall with a trellis decorated with climbing plants. The entrance is offstage to the right.

AT RISE, Cerise is seated counting money.

CERISE: 27, 28, 29, plus the 20 francs I just received from the store, that makes 30 gold pieces. Total: 600 francs.

(*Maman Fipart comes in from the back and stops to watch Cerise counting.*)

MAMAN FIPART: Well, Cerise, what is it that you are doing there?
CERISE (*quickly hiding the money*): Auntie! I'm counting what I earned this week.
MAMAN FIPART: Ah! You've been to the store to get your money. Well, what are you going to do with what you've earned, little one? Are you looking to buy a

dress? Or a bonnet? That's really being cautious, but (*laughing*) one your age shouldn't be miserly!

CERISE: Oh no, I'm not miserly, Auntie. If I keep on saving like this, it's to have a big splurge. Then I'll buy myself–

MAMAN FIPART: What?

CERISE: Oh! It's too embarrassing to tell.

MAMAN FIPART: Something very expensive to wear?

CERISE: I'm not a coquette, auntie.

MAMAN FIPART: Even to please Monsieur Jean?

(*Jean Guignon appears at the door at the back.*)

JEAN GUIGNON: I heard my name. Can I come in?

CERISE: Why, certainly. Come in, Monsieur Jean.

MAMAN FIPART: Come in, my boy.

(*Jean's head still bears the wound he received in the Prologue.*)

JEAN GUIGNON: Madame Fipart, may I present you my respects. Mademoiselle Cerise, I am indeed yours–if you don't see it as an inconvenience.

CERISE: Ah, how happy you seem today, Monsieur Jean.

JEAN GUIGNON: That's what I came here to tell you. I think I'm cured.

MAMAN FIPART (*who's seated herself at the left and taken up her work*): Truly?

JEAN GUIGNON: Word of honor! Since my last misadventure with that flower pot–that I told you about–six months ago, that was–well, since then, it seems to me that things are going much better. First of all, I haven't had a single man fall into my arms. That's a fact–and not

37

later than yesterday, a fire started in the house where I live, the entire house burned down, but I escaped totally unharmed. Also, things are picking up–business is good– I've got so many errands to run that I don't know where to stick my legs. Luck's smiling at me, finally!

CERISE: So much the better, Monsieur Jean. So much the better!

JEAN GUIGNON: That's what decided me to ask for something that I'd been putting off for a while. I said to myself–since bad luck is going away, perhaps happiness is going to come in–and then I made my decision.

MAMAN FIPART: Whom do you want to ask?

JEAN GUIGNON: Whom?

CERISE: Yes, whom?

JEAN GUIGNON (*aside*): Whom indeed? Hold on. I thought this would be simple and here I go, messing up things already. (*aloud*) Hum! Madame Fipart, I guess I should ask you first–since you are here. And you can help me nicely with my proposal.

MAMAN FIPART: Me?

JEAN GUIGNON: Yes, you. I would like to propose to a certain linen girl–but I don't know the proper forms and I wouldn't want risking being disrespectful–to her– or to you, for that matter.

MAMAN FIPART: I see. (*looking at Cerise who blushes and lowers her eyes*) And what is the name of this linen girl?

JEAN GUIGNON (*fumbling in his pocket*): Well, er... I can't tell you her name! I forgot the white gloves!

MAMAN FIPART: Are the white gloves really necessary?

JEAN GUIGNON: The boys I work with told me that one should always wear white gloves when proposing. Doesn't make any difference if they are silk or cotton, but one must wear white gloves. It's *de rigueur*. Oh! My tongue's itching enough. Today's not the first day I wanted to do it, but every time, I was afraid she'd say something like: "Monsieur Jean, you're a fine lad, not bad in your person and nice enough for a man–"

CERISE: That's true.

JEAN GUIGNON: So I'm told. But let me go on. She'd continue: "You want to set up a household–that's fine. But you have no money, the girl has no money–and two penniless fiancés put together make for a truly penniless marriage."

MAMAN FIPART: True enough.

JEAN GUIGNON: So you see–

MAMAN FIPART: But on the other hand, she might tell you: "Monsieur Jean, the love of work is the best and safest fortune." And then, there are also young misses who sometimes have dowries–secret dowries–isn't that so, Cerise?

CERISE (*without raising her head*): Yes, auntie, there are.

MAMAN FIPART: I know one such girl that will bring her husband–how much will she bring, Cerise?

CERISE: Six hundred francs, auntie!

JEAN GUIGNON (*astonished*): Six hundred francs. You know young girls who have 600 francs for a dowry?

MAMAN FIPART: Actually, Cerise is mistaken. The girl I know will bring 1,000 francs.

CERISE: No, no, I said 600.

MAMAN FIPART: I'm better informed than you.

JEAN GUIGNON: One *thousand* francs?

CERISE: One *thousand* francs!

MAMAN FIPART: Wouldn't that be a nice dowry, eh, Monsieur Jean?

JEAN GUIGNON: That'd be a *fortune*! But the dowry is nothing to me. It's the girl who's everything.

MAMAN FIPART: Well said! Go buy some white gloves, then, and return to make your proposal.

JEAN GUIGNON: Ah! You know that it is Mademoiselle Cerise whom I want to ask to marry me–with or without a dowry, and you consent? Ah! Madame Fipart! Dear Madame Fipart! Ah! Mademoiselle Cerise! You consent–truly?

CERISE: Will you go and buy your gloves!

JEAN GUIGNON: Yes, yes! I'm going! You must understand–I'm not accustomed to success. My head is spinning. I'm having flashes. Oh! I think I'm going to faint.

CERISE: I hope not.

JEAN GUIGNON: No, no. It's passed, it's passed off! Oh! Madame Fipart, Mademoiselle Cerise, I'll buy the finest, softest white leather gloves in all of Paris.

(*Jean rushes to the door and knocks over Tulipe who holds a watering can.*)

TULIPE: Ah! Did I hurt you?

JEAN GUIGNON: Not at all! Not at all! Everything is going great for me. I'm lucky, I'm so lucky!

(*He leaves, running.*)

TULIPE: What's got into him? Has he gone mad! (*She continues to water plants*)

CERISE: Oh! Auntie, my good auntie!

MAMAN FIPART: Why, you sly girl! You worked industriously all by yourself and managed to save 600 francs. Darn! As for me–I've done what I could.

CERISE: You're like a mother to me, auntie! God knows what privations you've endured to save those 400 francs you've so generously given me.

MAMAN FIPART: Shut up, little goose! Doesn't an aunt have the right to dower her niece? (*sadly*) At least, you–you love me!

CERISE: Yes, I love you, auntie. Here, see how much I love you. (*She hugs and kisses her*)

MAMAN FIPART: Dear child.

TULIPE (*coming forward*): Heavens! They're kissing in my courtyard now! Well, just go about your business as if I wasn't here!

MAMAN FIPART (*happily*): Come on! Don't be cross, Madame Tulipe! We will invite you to the wedding, my dear landlady. Now I'm going to collect all our work because I don't think we're going to do any more work today.

(*She goes inside to the left.*)

TULIPE: A wedding? You're getting married? To whom?

CERISE: Jean Guignon.

TULIPE: So much the better! At least, I won't have just single folks living in my house. (*Cerise laughs*) Yes, you and I, two young women on this side (*she points to the left*) and here, (*pointing to the right*) Monsieur Albert and Monsieur Alphonse, two confirmed bachelors–too many single folks under one roof. I don't like it. It's not proper. Monsieur Albert is quite proper.

TULIPE: He, yes. Besides, he spends half his time outside, giving art lessons–but the other...

CERISE (*laughing*): Monsieur Alphonse, the lawyer!

TULIPE: Oh! That one! He can take pride being the most awful tenant I ever had. Every time he sees me, he asks me for money for repairs. If I listened to him, I'd be ruined.

(*We hear the sounds of a carriage.*)

CERISE: Heavens! A carriage is stopping outside.
TULIPE (*going to look*): Oh, a pretty calèche! A beautiful lady's getting out. Ah! what a beautiful dress!

(*Baccarat enters.*)

BACCARAT: I'm looking for Monsieur Albert–
TULIPE: This is the right place, Madame.
BACCARAT: Is he home?
TULIPE: No, Madame. He went out!
BACCARAT: Out! Ah! (*to herself*) He's beginning to forget me. (*aloud, after having looked at Tulipe and Cerise attentively*) Why, if I'm not mistaken, could it be you? Tulipe! Cerise!
CERISE: You know us?
BACCARAT: Yes, of course, I know you! Have I really changed that much, that you haven't already said "Hello, Louisette." (*giving her hand to Tulipe*) Yes, your old neighbor from the Rue des Fossés du Temple.
CERISE: Louisette! We haven't seen you for–what?– five years? It *is* you! (*getting hold of herself*) It really is you!
BACCARAT (*offering her hand as well*): You said it, my dear Cerise, it really is me.
TULIPE: How have you been? Are you married? You must have married a Senator.

BACCARAT: No, I'm not married. But let's speak of you, my friends. What became of you after we lost sight of each other?

TULIPE: As for me, I inherited some money and bought this house, so now I'm a landlady. The house, the land, the trees, the flowers–all are mine, and I've just watered my own string beans.

BACCARAT: What about you, Cerise?

CERISE: Oh! I'm rich. I have a 1,000 francs dowry and I'm marrying a fine lad whom I love with all my heart.

BACCARAT (*with a sigh*): I see you both have had good fortune. It's good to know.

TULIPE: Well, what about you? If, as they say, life's a lottery, you look like you won the grand prize.

BACCARAT: Yes, I have a carriage, a mansion, furs, jewels. My horses are amongst the finest in Paris, my dresses the most elegant. I am rich, very rich...

CERISE: That's funny! You couldn't inherit your fortune from your family, because if I remember correctly, it consisted only of an old uncle who was a tinkerer...

BACCARAT: No, I didn't inherit my fortune.

TULIPE: Then, how did you get all that?

BACCARAT: It was given to me.

TULIPE: Given?

BACCARAT: And, it cost me dearly, too. When the rest of you go out, with your little dresses and your little bonnets, no one points a finger at you. You, Cerise, they call "Mademoiselle Bertin" and they salute you. You, Tulipe, "Mademoiselle Hubert" and they salute you. Me, they call–

CERISE: Mademoiselle Charmet, and they salute you, too.

BACCARAT: No. They call me "La Baccarat" and they do not salute me.

(*The two girls recoil.*)

BACCARAT: "Baccarat!" Why that nickname rather than another? I don't know–but today that name is known throughout Paris–and not by the Paris which works honestly for a living, but by the idle Paris which only seeks to entertain itself.

TULIPE: I've heard the name. They say, "beautiful as Baccarat," "elegant as Baccarat."

BACCARAT: And they also say, "infamous as Baccarat!"

TULIPE: Ah! No! No–

CERISE: Poor Louisette!

BACCARAT: My story, you see, is like that of all these poor girls, whose heart is gnawed by envy and who tire of working for a pitiful salary, but honestly earned, salary. Girls transported as in a fairy tale from their wretched garrets to a splendid apartment, covered with lace and jewels, seeing the most handsome names throw themselves at their feet, the greatest fortunes of France. At first, such girls think themselves queens to be adored, but in truth, they're only slaves who are paid. They awaken one day, at the first insult thrown at them, and see themselves, such as they are; they blush at the dazzle surrounding them, but by then, it's too late. One can never climb back up that slope–one can only keep going down–always down. Then, oh, then they cast away, far away, the memory of their past. They numb themselves to their Hell, and when the shame becomes too great, too unbearable, they start using their fortune to crush those honest women who shame them with their modesty and virtue. And to those men of the world who've brought them that shame, they bring ruin. Pay, they say, keep on paying; we were adorned with diamonds, we intend to be covered with them; we had mansions, we must have palaces. Pay, pay, forever! And they give us whatever we ask for. Yes, we've got everything, except the esteem of others and our own self-esteem.

CERISE: Ah, Louisette–why did you leave us?

BACCARAT: Oh! You don't yet know the full extent of my suffering. You're in love; soon, you'll become the wife of the one your heart has freely chosen; he will be proud of you. I, too, am in love, with all the strength of my soul, but the one I love will never become my husband, will never be proud of me... I've already been lucky that Albert even wanted to be seen with me.

CERISE: Monsieur Albert? Is he the one you love?

TULIPE: Oh! He can't but love you: you're so beautiful!

BACCARAT: I haven't seen him for a week, and during all of that week, I've been weeping. He is ignoring me, rejecting me perhaps. Maybe, he loves another.

CERISE: That's impossible!

BACCARAT (*crying and letting herself fall into a chair*): Oh! If that's the case, I'd die. Yes, I know I'd die of it.

(*Sir Williams, i.e.Andrea, enters, followed by Venture, dressed as a footman.*)

SIR WILLIAMS: Why, indeed, it's really her carriage! She must be here!

BACCARAT (*rising quickly*): Someone's coming! Oh– they mustn't see me cry. Girls like me can't be seen to cry. (*to Andrea*) Sir Williams. Why, what a surprise.

SIR WILLIAMS: Baccarat. What are you doing here?

BACCARAT: Same as you, it seems. Checking on young Albert. But he's out.

SIR WILLIAMS: The Devil! It's bad luck to make such a useless trip, and on a racing day, too!

BACCARAT: If you want a place in my carriage, I'll be happy to take you (*smiling wickedly*) I mean, to Paris.

SIR WILLIAMS: No, thank you. I have my coupé. (*pause*) Well, since I'm in Belleville, I might as well wait for the return of your young friend.

BACCARAT (*falsely light*): If you see him, tell him I'll be at home this evening—I'd like him to drop by.

SIR WILLIAMS: I will do so. In return, I have something to ask of you.

BACCARAT: Of me?

SIR WILLIAMS: Yes. The favor of introducing you this evening to a charming young man, a friend of mine recently arrived from the Indies to take possession of a fortune estimated at five millions francs. I warn you, my beautiful siren, that my friend is also coming to get married. So don't go making him forget that!

BACCARAT: 'Till this evening then. (*to the girls*) Bye, dear ones.

TULIPE (*whispering to Baccarat*): Do you have to leave?

BACCARAT: Yes! You heard Sir Williams. Today's a racing day—and I must be seen there.

TULIPE: Well, then—goodbye!

CERISE (*joining them*): No—wait! When you—if you get bored—tired of your life, remember Tulipe and Cerise who will always receive you well and console you—and call you "Mademoiselle Charmet."

BACCARAT (*moved to hug them both*): Thank you! Thank you, dear ones!

TULIPE: I'll walk you to your carriage.

CERISE: And I'll go and see what auntie is doing.
BACCARAT: Goodbye, Sir Williams.
SIR WILLIAMS: 'Till later, Baccarat.

(*Baccarat leaves by the rear with Tulipe; Cerise goes inside to the right.*)

SIR WILLIAMS: Are we alone?
VENTURE: Yes! But let's not forget that Maman Fipart lives here, no doubt still crying over her fine son who disappeared these many months ago.
SIR WILLIAMS: She must have received–or will soon receive–the letter which Rocambole wrote to her according to my wishes–a letter that one of our associates, leaving for Mexico, carried with him with instructions to mail it from Havana. Madame Fipart now believes–or will soon believe–that her son has gone to seek fortune in the New World. So we shan't occupy ourselves further with her. You haven't given me an account of your trip yesterday. Is our business finally complete?
VENTURE: When you left Paris, six months ago, the day after the death of the old Marquis de Chamery, you ordered me to disband the Club of the Jack of Hearts. It was a difficult thing to do; they all objected; some even accused you of deserting them. But in the end, it was done just as you ordered. Today, the Club of the Jack of Hearts no longer exists. I sent your share of the loot to the secret retreat where you'd gone to shut yourself up from the world with the lad you nearly killed.
SIR WILLIAMS: Fortunately, before stabbing, I saw his face. I then realized that to get hold of the Chamery fortune, I needed a young man, one originating from such humble beginnings as to be virtually unknown in

the Parisian society—a man who, above all, could be my creature, completely mine. Rocambole was just that man. A few minor assaults, some swindling, had barely brought him to the attention of the Police, Still, he would eventually have been arrested if his lucky star hadn't placed him across my path. I've carefully kept the official documents which, if I so desire, can prove his identity and which will enable me to remind him, should he ever forget, that he's only Joseph Fipart. I worked hard to transform him and prepare him to play the role I have chosen for him. It was a complete education, but the lad proved admirably gifted, a prodigious student. Today, Rocambole writes and speaks like a gentleman; he handles weapons like Grisier, mounts a horse like Baucher, knows English like a Lord; India like Mey, and Paris like all our press chroniclers put together.

VENTURE: You accomplished all that in just six months?

SIR WILLIAMS: What can I say? That lad doesn't learn, he divines. Meanwhile, you have used that time profitably to further my plan. The money you've sent me enabled me to credibly assume the identity of Sir Williams, an old friend of the Marquis de Chamery, who will eventually become a millionaire five times over, and that without counting the fortune of the Sallandreras, which also can't escape me.

VENTURE: I followed your instructions to the letter, Master. When you arrived in Paris two weeks ago, you found a suite at the Grand Hotel at your disposal. You were received like a nabob, and I gather that some Russian Comte you met there immediately introduced you to the beautiful Baccarat, Queen of the demimonde.

SIR WILLIAMS: That was a lucky break! That worthy Prince has unknowingly done me a great service. Do you know whom I met at Baccarat's? A young man whom I suspect might in fact be the true heir of the noble family of Chamery.

VENTURE: The Devil you say!

SIR WILLIAMS: As you can guess, that, if my suspicions become certitude, you will have a further role to play...

VENTURE: Who is this young man?

SIR WILLIAMS: Silence! Here he is. Go wait for me outside.

(*Venture leaves just as Tulipe returns, accompanied by Albert de Chamery, who carries a package.*)

TULIPE: Yes, Monsieur Albert, you missed the beautiful lady by five minutes; but a gentleman has been waiting for you. Wait, here he is.

(*The two men bow to each other. Tulipe leaves by the left carrying her water can.*)

ALBERT: Why, it seems to me, Monsieur, that I've already had the honor of being introduced to you.

SIR WILLIAMS: Indeed. We met twice at Baccarat's.

ALBERT: You are the Baronet Sir Williams, right?

SIR WILLIAMS: I thank you for doing me the honor of remembering my name.

ALBERT: And you've had the courage to clamber to the heights of Belleville to see me?

SIR WILLIAMS: That won't surprise you when you learn that I've come to ask you a service.

ALBERT: A service? From me?

SIR WILLIAMS: I don't know what you know about me, Monsieur. I am English and rich–my intention is to settle here, in Paris. I've already bought a mansion. I'd like to decorate it properly now, and I've come to beg you to paint me a picture. At Baccarat's, I saw some of your sketches–truly remarkable, featuring landscapes from Ireland, of the Bengal. You're Irish, but you've traveled to India?

ALBERT: Indeed, I'm coming from India, Monsieur, but I'm not Irish. I'm French.

SIR WILLIAMS: Really? Of a noble or bourgeois family?

ALBERT: Alas, I don't know my real name. I was raised by my old nurse who died before my return to Europe.

SIR WILLIAMS: Even today, you are unaware of your father's name?

ALBERT: I'm ignorant of it.

SIR WILLIAMS: And, you have no indication, no clue which could permit you one day to find your family?

ALBERT (*after having looked at him, intrigued*): No, I have not!

SIR WILLIAMS (*aside*): I breathe easier. (*aloud*) Romantic stories like these are rare in the times in which we live. But what you've just told me adds to my interest in you. Monsieur Albert, I am counting on a painting.

ALBERT: I will start tomorrow.

SIR WILLIAMS (*after having looked at his watch*): The races must have begun. I will have the pleasure of seeing you again soon at Baccarat's?

ALBERT: Yes, I'll be there. (*aside*) For the last time.

SIR WILLIAMS (*aside*): No immediate danger there. Still, I shouldn't lose sight of him. (*aloud*) Until then, Monsieur. At Baccarat's.

ARMAND (*bowing*): Au revoir, Monsieur.

(Sir Williams leaves by the rear just when Alphonse appears. Alphonse steps aside to let him pass.)

ALPHONSE: Excuse me, Monsieur.

(Sir William bows to Alphonse and leaves.)

ALPHONSE: *Mordieu*! A gentleman in a coupé, Rue des Moulins in Belleville. Wonders will never cease. Who did he come to see, I wonder?
ALBERT: He came to see me!
ALPHONSE: Indeed? Why, here you are, making it into the high society! And our landlady who complains of having starving artists and shysters squat her house!
ALBERT: You're too modest. You're an attorney.
ALPHONSE: Yes, an attorney still waiting for his first case, whereas you, handsome devil, you're the preferred lover of La Baccarat, the Queen of Paris, and the distinguished teacher of the Señorita Concepcion de Sallandrera, an Infante of Spain!
ALBERT: Who told you that?
ALPHONSE: Play at being mysterious! I know everything! Dare you deny that, since you've had the honor of giving lessons to the Señorita, you've fallen in love with her? Which is why you've been neglecting the delectable Baccarat?
ALBERT: Shut up, you scoundrel!
ALPHONSE: Deny it, I dare you! Go on, give me the lie! I dare you! *(laughter)* You see, I practice in private life.
ALBERT: Well, yes, you've spoken the truth. But my love for Concepcion is a mad dream! And fools are to be pitied, my friend, not made fun of.

(Albert takes his package and his hat, which he had placed on a chair.)

ALPHONSE: From the moment you confess, you're already acquitted. Where are you going?
ALBERT: Back to work!
ALPHONSE: And to think of her!
ALBERT: Later!
ALPHONSE: Later!

(Albert goes to his room.)

ALPHONSE: Oh, love! Love! Terrible disease which starts in the heart and ends either at Clichy or in a Marriage. I, too, am sick. For I am in love with Mademoiselle Tulipe, our pretty landlady.

(Tulipe returns.)

TULIPE *(aside)*: Monsieur Alphonse. Great! I'm going to be bored again.
ALPHONSE *(aside)*: Here she is. *(aloud)* You're no doubt surprised to see me at this hour, Mademoiselle Tulipe. If I've returned so soon from the Courthouse, if I've torn myself from my many clients, it's because I had to speak to you about some urgent business.
TULIPE: That's it! There you are again, asking me for repair money.
ALPHONSE: Mademoiselle, all my chimney flues need sweeping!
TULIPE: You have only one stove.
ALPHONSE: It smokes like four. Moreover, my wall paper is wrinkling, fading... It's turned from its original red to yellow.

TULIPE: A new wallpaper! I put it up not even two months ago.

ALPHONSE: That's because it was cheap, of bad quality! I request a new wallpaper or I shall sue.

TULIPE: Sue me?

ALPHONSE: Come, I only ask for an amicable settlement. Then I promise to never ask for anything more–but on one condition.

TULIPE: So long as it doesn't cost me any money.

ALPHONSE: Come and have dinner with me this Sunday at Bougival.

TULIPE: Monsieur Alphonse!

ALPHONSE: That's my demand! Bougival or the tribunal!

TULIPE: Well–

ALPHONSE: Well?

TULIPE: If we can convince Cerise to accompany us with Monsieur Jean and Madame Fipart, I will go along with your proposal–out of a sense of thrift, of course.

ALPHONSE: Very well! They'll be so much easier to convince since today is the day of the boat races. But by mentioning Madame Fipart, you just reminded me that I have a rather unpleasant message for that lady.

TULIPE: For Madame Fipart?

ALPHONSE: Yes! Go, my charming landlady, and remember our agreement.

TULIPE: I will, but I warn you–if you come up with any more demands, I will give you notice! I'll go and re-iron my green dress.

ALPHONSE: Ah! She is charming.

(*Tulipe leaves. Maman Fipart appears.*)

ALPHONSE: I was going to come and see you, my dear Madame Fipart.

MAMAN FIPART: See me? What for?

ALPHONSE: First, you must arm yourself with courage and composure.

MAMAN FIPART: Courage? Composure? Monsieur Alphonse, do you have bad news to give me? Is it about my son?

ALPHONSE: I'm afraid it is.

MAMAN FIPART: Is he ill? Oh no! I can barely bring myself to listen to you.

(*At this time, Cerise appears at one of the windows on the ground floor.*)

CERISE (*aside*): What can Monsieur Alphonse be telling my aunt? (*she listens*)

ALPHONSE: Madame Fipart, six or seven months ago, your son committed some petty crimes.

MAMAN FIPART (*her hand clutching at her heart*): Ah!

ALPHONSE: Nothing too serious, mind you! But still, the man from whom he, er, borrowed, some might say "embezzled," a not inconsequential sum of money has just notified me that he's tired of waiting for repayment and now plans to–

MAMAN FIPART: ...To sue.

ALPHONSE: Worse. To file a complaint with the Police.

MAMAN FIPART (*hiding her head in her hands*): Ah! My God! My God!

ALPHONSE: If he does, your son might be–

MAMAN FIPART: Convicted! Dishonored! That's why he's been missing for the last seven months. He's afraid the Police will come looking for him here.

ALPHONSE: The plaintiff, however, is willing to not go to court if the money is promptly repaid.

MAMAN FIPART: How much are we talking about?

ALPHONSE: My understanding is that it's in the neighborhood of 1200 francs.

MAMAN FIPART: Twelve hundred francs! That much! Oh! My God! ...But then, it could buy his life back... (*as if struck by an idea*) Monsieur Alphonse, what about a repayment plan? If you were to approach this man with a repayment schedule, would he be satisfied with that?

ALPHONSE: I could try. How much would you offer to pay, and how often?

MAMAN FIPART: Ah, poor Cerise!... Offer him 400 francs now, then the same every quarter!

ALPHONSE: That's not much to start...

(*Cerise emerges from the house.*)

CERISE: Then offer him 1000 francs.

MAMAN FIPART: Ah! Cerise! My poor child! What about your dowry?

CERISE: Jean will wait.

(*Jean Guignon, now wearing gloves, appears at the back.*)

JEAN GUIGNON: Hello! I don't know what you're talking about, but I can't wait. These gloves are murder on my hands! Madame Fipart, I'm back and I have the honor of having the privilege of asking you, if it doesn't inconvenience you in any way, for the hand of

55

Mademoiselle Cerise, hereby present–with whom I have the honor of being deeply in love–in marriage. I am, Madame, your most humble and respectful nephew. Well? You don't say anything? (*looking at Cerise who's weeping*) And you are crying, Mademoiselle Cerise? Madame Fipart, is it that you don't want me? Has my bad luck returned?

CERISE: It has, Jean; we can no longer marry this year.

JEAN GUIGNON: Why?

CERISE: Because I no longer have a dowry.

JEAN GUIGNON: Dowry, no dowry, it's all the same to me. I'll take you without one.

CERISE: That's impossible, Monsieur Jean!

JEAN GUIGNON (*letting himself fall into a chair*): Ah! The flower pot was less painful! I'm choking! I, who was so happy just now, who ran so fast to return faster... (*pulling out his handkerchief and letting two letters fall from his pocket*) This morning, I laughed, tonight, I cry!

ALPHONSE: Come on, Monsieur Jean, console yourself. You won't lose much by waiting another year. Come, put your handkerchief back in your pocket, and pick up these two letters you just dropped!

JEAN GUIGNON: What letters? Ah! yes! These two! The mailman just gave them to me. There's one for Monsieur Albert, from India–and the other comes from almost as far–and it's for you, Madame Fipart.

MAMAN FIPART: For me?

JEAN GUIGNON: Here, Monsieur Alphonse, take this letter to Monsieur Albert. Perhaps it's an inheritance from over there. That's the way life is: pain for some, happiness for others...

(*Alphonse takes the letter and goes to Albert's room.*)

JEAN GUIGNON: As to the other... Are you thinking of going into the cigar trade, Madame Fipart? It comes from Havana.

MAMAN FIPART: From Havana?

JEAN GUIGNON: Straight from there. See–it says so on the yellow stamp.

MAMAN FIPART (*taking the letter*): Ah! It's from Joseph! It's from my son!

CERISE: From him!

JEAN GUIGNON: Probably looking for some fake Havanas to resell as real ones.

MAMAN FIPART (*reading*): "My dear mother, I intend to reform myself. I have gone to the West Indies and will stay there until I've made my fortune. For that I will need some luck– and time; that's why I beg you to forget that you have a son. I will return rich or not at all. Your little Joseph a.k.a. Rocambole." (*letting the letter fall*) Gone! Gone forever! (*collapsing into a chair*) I no longer have a son!

(*They all surround Maman Fipart who weeps.*)

CERISE: But I'm still here with you, I am.

(*At this time, Albert appears on the landing, rereading the letter he's just received. Alphonse follows him.*)

ALBERT (*happy*): To Marseille! Major Gordon–a name, at last! A fortune! O Concepcion! At last I will be worthy of you!

CURTAIN

ACT II

Scene II

An elegant smoking room at Baccarat's.

FANNY (*settled on a divan, and looking in a mirror*):
Straighten up the room, Baptiste, and carefully. Madame
will be having company this evening.
BAPTISTE: Pah! A smoking room in the home of a
single woman! (*looking at the clock*) The races will soon
be over.
FANNY: Madame will have dined at La Marche. (*sound
of a clock*) Ah! The bells.
BAPTISTE: Company's coming.
FANNY (*rising*): So soon! Go light the salon quickly.

(*Sir Williams enters.*)

SIR WILLIAMS (*to Baptiste*): No need, my good man. I
will be very comfortable here waiting for your mistress–
and a friend whom I mean to introduce to her.
BAPTISTE (*aside*): That's the Baronet whom the
Russian Comte brought last week.
SIR WILLIAMS: Go. Go about your work.
BAPTISTE (*aside*): I seem to annoy the milord.
SIR WILLIAMS (*to Fanny*): But you may stay, my little
one.
BAPTISTE (*aside*): He doesn't fool me. I see his game.
He's going to bribe Fanny. Now there's a girl who
knows how to feather her own nest.

(Baptiste leaves.)

SIR WILLIAMS (*stretching out in an armchair*): Give me a light, child.

FANNY: Yes, My Lord.

SIR WILLIAMS: Thank you! Do you know how sweet you are! But your lovely curly hair could use a comb. Here, that should buy you a pretty one.

FANNY: Five francs?

SIR WILLIAMS: Nice of me, isn't it? I haven't compensated you for your warm welcome, little one. Would you like to help me? To really help me? Would you promise not to refuse anything I might ask of you?

FANNY: Ah! My Lord–

SIR WILLIAMS: Two combs would really suit your hair better, don't you think? Right now, you've got enough money to buy only, but that can be remedied... Here!

FANNY: Another five francs!

SIR WILLIAMS: Can I count on you now?

FANNY: Oh yes, My Lord! But I wouldn't want you to waste your money and be angry later. I guess you want me to put in a good word for you in Madame's ears. I've got to tell you, since I've been in her service, she's entertained half of Paris, but has listened to no one but herself. I understand she's in love with Monsieur Albert–a fine young man–and isn't interested in any other man...

SIR WILLIAMS: You let me be the judge of what I want, pretty one. I want only want you to do my bidding when I ask. Worry not about the results.

FANNY: I won't be ungrateful, My Lord.

SIR WILLIAMS: I hope so. And I always pay in advance, too.

(*Baptiste returns.*)

BAPTISTE: There's a young gentleman asking for you, My Lord.

SIR WILLIAMS: Ah! That must be the friend I was expecting. Show him in!

(*Fanny and Baptiste leave. Rocambole enters, elegantly dressed.*)

SIR WILLIAMS: Come closer. (*looking at him*) Fine. That outfit is almost perfect. And you're on time, too.

ROCAMBOLE: Too much so, it seems. I gather Baccarat hasn't returned yet?

SIR WILLIAMS: So much the better. That leaves us time to chat. Did Venture bring you here?

ROCAMBOLE: Yes.

SIR WILLIAMS: You owe that man a lot.

ROCAMBOLE: I know. If, six months ago, he hadn't arrived just as you were about to– (*makes the gesture of stabbing someone*)

SIR WILLIAMS: Upon my word, without him you were a dead man.

ROCAMBOLE: My life wasn't worth much at the time– no question about it–still, I'd have missed it.

SIR WILLIAMS: Do you know why I let you live that night?

ROCAMBOLE: Well, you did make me swear to obey you blindly and not to ask you a single question. But now that we're back in Paris, that you've taught me so much, I guess the time is right for you to tell me, isn't it, my good Master?

SIR WILLIAMS: Indeed it is.

ROCAMBOLE: I thought so.

SIR WILLIAMS: Sit down. Take a cigar and listen. Oh! This is a great story! You're going to love it!

ROCAMBOLE (*lighting up*): I'm moved already.

SIR WILLIAMS: Are you making fun of me?

ROCAMBOLE: Not at all. I can't help it. I've always been prone to make fun of things, especially when they're serious. I know it's a bad habit. Please excuse me, my good Master. I am listening.

SIR WILLIAMS: So you want to know why I spared your miserable life?

ROCAMBOLE: I do.

SIR WILLIAMS: To make you a millionaire, a Marquis whose lineage stretches back to the Crusades, and after that, marry you to the daughter of a Grandee of Spain!

ROCAMBOLE: You–you must be joking?

SIR WILLIAMS: I've never been more serious.

ROCAMBOLE: Then, you truly have the power to make miracles, like the *djinn* that came out of that lamp in that Arabian fairy tale you made me read.

SIR WILLIAMS: I am a bit of a miracle-worker, indeed. Once, I was a poor devil, just like you. I wanted to be rich, to be powerful. I thought gambling would be my path to a better world. So I began playing in the salons, but then, I also lost. So I learned how to trick fate, to force luck to smile on me. I became very good at it, until one night, misfortune, or rather clumsiness, made me drop one of the cards I was hiding up my sleeve, and that in front of everyone. My opponent picked up the card, called me a cheat, then proceeded to thrash me within an inch of my life and had me thrown out in the gutter.

ROCAMBOLE: You killed him?

SIR WILLIAMS: I could not, not there, not then. I had to bide my time. But that fateful card I was hiding that night–a Jack of Hearts–was found, six months later, nailed to his chest by a dagger. It's that same card that they began to find everywhere a crime had been committed, for I became the leader of a formidable gang of thieves and murderers that all Paris knew as the Club of the Jack of Hearts. The City lived in fear of us–but one tires of everything, even of being a villain. I had accumulated a vast fortune; I was now powerful beyond belief; yet I began to weary of the struggle. I planned to retire to America when luck threw me one last marvelous piece of business. I told you the story of the Marquis de Chamery, and of his son who was languishing miserably in India?

ROCAMBOLE: Yes.

SIR WILLIAMS: At first, I intended to go and find this young man, and tell him the news, in return for sharing that immense fortune which he didn't know was coming to him. But I chanced upon a more amusing possibility–why travel halfway across the globe to find someone, and risk being disappointed, when I could manufacture an almost identical someone at home.

ROCAMBOLE: I confess I don't follow.

SIR WILLIAMS: You will. It pleased me not to go to India to try to locate the son of the Marquis de Chamery, but to take one Joseph Fipart, alias Rocambole, who was mine, completely mine, and remake him into the son of the old Marquis. And when you've taken possession of your title and your vast inheritance, when you are the son-in-law of the Duke de Sallandrera and a Grandee of Spain, then we will settle our accounts.

ROCAMBOLE: Me! Noble, rich and a Grandee of Spain!

SIR WILLIAMS: Yes, but you'll still be Rocambole underneath it all–at least, when I wish it. Remember the Arabian tales I made you read? Aladdin was a beggar and a common thief until he found the magic lamp, and then he became a Prince and traded his bed of filth for one made of gold and silk. But when he lost the lamp, he became a beggar again. You do remember that?

ROCAMBOLE: Actually, the Sorcerer took the lamp away from him.

SIR WILLIAMS: Exactly. Aladdin betrayed his Master and as punishment, was cast back to live among the offals. Take another cigar–you let yours go out!

ROCAMBOLE: It's true! (*aside*) Ah! Now there's a willful man I better not cross.

SIR WILLIAMS: We'll say that you came from India where I went to find you, armed with the will of Monsieur de Chamery–your noble father–and other documents proving your noble birth. Tonight, you will make your entry into the Parisian *demimonde*; at your age, and with your fortune, it's the way one should start. In a few days, I will introduce you to the Duke de Sallandrera who is waiting for you to give you his daughter's hand in marriage.

ROCAMBOLE: Whatever you ask of me, my good Master, it will never be enough for me to repay you for your kindness.

SIR WILLIAMS: That's the spirit. (*sound of horses*) Ah, I gather the Queen of this palace has returned. By the way, there will be some gambling tonight. I've asked Venture to fill your wallet.

ROCAMBOLE: Yes. There are 15 francs in there, I believe.

SIR WILLIAMS (*sighing*): Venture is an imbecile! You'll need 15,000 francs. You have no ideas of the stakes they play for here. One night, Comte Artoff, who introduced me to this place, played a game of baccarat with the Mistress of the House herself. He suggested as a wager a trip to Italy against 100,000 francs. If the lady lost, she promised to accompany the Comte to Italy–and be faithful to him for three months. If he lost, she would win 100,000 francs. The Comte lost, begged for another game and promptly lost again. And so on. In short, that night, the woman won 600,000 francs and her nickname: La Baccarat. But she was a good sport and graciously agreed to the trip to Italy that he hadn't won. What a gesture! So you see, my dear fellow, that your 15 francs will be a pittance here. Your carriage is here, here's my key, run to my house and take 15 or 20,000 francs from my desk.

ROCAMBOLE (*aside*): I'll see if there's anything else in that desk.

SIR WILLIAMS: And return quickly.

(*Exit Rocambole. Enter Baccarat with Fanny.*)

BACCARAT: Fanny, relieve me of this.

(*She takes off her hat which she gives to Fanny, who leaves.*)

BACCARAT: A thousand pardons, Sir Williams, for not having been here to greet you. Oh, what a boring thing these races are! I thought they'd never end.

SIR WILLIAMS: Did you bet?

BACCARAT: I should think so.

SIR WILLIAMS: Did you win?

BACCARAT: I always do. Have you seen Monsieur Albert? Is he coming this evening?

SIR WILLIAMS: I have seen him and he'll come.

(*Fanny returns.*)

FANNY: Madame, Monsieur de Chateau Milly, the Marquis Van Hop and the Comte Artoff have just arrived.

BACCARAT: Already?

SIR WILLIAMS: Poor Artoff. Have you completely abandoned him now? You haven't kept any tender memories of your time together?

BACCARAT (*coldly*): The past is dead, Monsieur.

SIR WILLIAMS: I apologize for my clumsiness; I will go and join these gentlemen, and tell them that you're dressing. Thus, you'll be able to receive the one you're waiting for in full privacy.

BACCARAT (*smiling*): Thank you.

SIR WILLIAMS: You've forgiven me for my *gaffe* then?

BACCARAT (*extending her hand to him*): Of course.

(*Sir Williams kisses her hand and leaves by the right.*)

BACCARAT: Quick, quick, Fanny, readjust my hair. My features are not too tired? I'm not too ugly?

FANNY (*adjusting Baccarat's hair*): Madame is as lovely as ever.

BACCARAT: Oh! I want to be beautiful for him. He's going to come, Fanny. It's been like a century since I've seen him.

FANNY: A week at most.

BACCARAT: A whole week without him—were it only an hour. Oh! I'm really going to scold him. No—that might frighten him and he wouldn't be back then.

(*Baptiste enters.*)

BAPTISTE (*announcing*): Monsieur Albert.

BACCARAT: Him! It's him. Don't let anyone else come in here.

(*Fanny and Baptiste leave as Albert enters.*)

BACCARAT: There you are, Monsieur. I had to go to Belleville to find you and yet you were not to be found even at home. Where were you?

ALBERT: I was giving a private lesson.

BACCARAT: A private lesson–to whom? Ah! I warn you: I am jealous of your students and your models.

ALBERT: Baccarat!

BACCARAT: You're right! You're right! I'm being silly. No scene tonight. No, I'm truly happy to see you again! What's wrong with you? Your hand is burning– and I find you pale, my dearest. You work too much...

ALBERT: I had to deliver a painting to Monsieur Durand-Ruel...

BACCARAT: Another masterpiece. Yes, a masterpiece for which they paid you little, as always. I wish you wouldn't sell your pictures–except to me.

ALBERT: You know, my darling, that I cannot sell anything to you.

BACCARAT: Yes, I forget that, with you and you alone, I have no right to be rich. Oh! Heavens, my fortune is what separates us. If I sometimes curse your scruples– but no, I respect them. My heart can still understand the delicacy of your feelings. O my Albert! If only I'd known you sooner... You see, my past, my abominable past–I wish I had the power to erase it, even if it cost me all that I possess. O my Albert! If you loved me as I love you, we could still be happy–yes, really happy. Say the word, and there'll no longer be anything between us–no fortune, no past. I will sell everything I own–or give it all to the poor! Albert, repentance, charity purifies. Then I'll become again what I once was: a honest girl. We will go far, very far away from here, so that no echo of Paris will reach us. And then, and then–I wish for nothing more, except honest work and love.

ALBERT: Poor Baccarat!

BACCARAT: Why are you weeping, listening to me?

ALBERT: I see that you really love me, and yet I am here to tell you–

(*Sir Williams returns.*)

SIR WILLIAMS: Many apologies, but there's some disturbance in the grand salon–and they asked me to go and fetch you.

BACCARAT: Ah! I have company, curse them. (*to Sir Williams*) Go tell them that I'm ill, dying, dead if you'd like. (*to Albert*) I no longer wish to live, except for you.

SIR WILLIAMS: You're not serious?

ALBERT: No, she is not. Baccarat owes it to her guests to make an appearance. As for me, I would like to have a few words with you, Sir Williams. On the subject of the painting you've ordered.

SIR WILLIAMS: By all means.

BACCARAT (*anxious*): I shan't be gone for long.

ALBERT: Take your time.

BACCARAT: 'Till later then. (*aside*) Shall he still be here when I return?

(*She leaves.*)

SIR WILLIAMS: We're alone now, my young friend. I wager it's not of that painting you wish to speak to me about?

ALBERT: You are right, Monsieur. I would like to ask you to give this letter to Baccarat.

SIR WILLIAMS: A letter... Something serious?

ALBERT: My goodbyes, forever. I came here–

SIR WILLIAMS: To speak with Baccarat whom you don't love, and courage failed you.

ALBERT: Yes.

SIR WILLIAMS: So what you mightn't have dared say to her, you wrote in that letter.

ALBERT: Yes. I'm telling her of my intentions to leave Paris.

SIR WILLIAMS: A transparent subterfuge, if you don't mind my saying so, which may not fool her for long.

ALBERT: But it is the truth! I leave tomorrow for Marseille.

SIR WILLIAMS: Are you that desperate to flee Baccarat that you plan to return to India?

ALBERT: Not at all. Since your earlier visit to Belleville, an event of considerable importance happened.

SIR WILLIAMS: Ah so?

ALBERT: When one has endured great suffering for a long time, and when suddenly an unhoped-for happy event occurs, one must share the news of that even with someone. Because you've shown me the kindness to take an interest in my life, I will tell you that I go to Marseille to meet a man who will, at long last, reveal to me the identity of my father.

SIR WILLIAMS (*surprised*): What?

ALBERT: An illustrious name, a princely fortune, that's what this person is supposed to tell me–if I provide him with the evidence he seeks.

SIR WILLIAMS: Evidence? What evidence? You told me you had no such thing.

ALBERT: Well, the good woman who raised me was given something by my mother before we were torn apart–a medallion.

SIR WILLIAMS: A medallion?

ALBERT: In it is a portrait of my mother. This is the only evidence I have. This is what this man–this Major Gordon who's arrived from India and is waiting for me at the Hotel des Ambassadeurs–is demanding to see.

SIR WILLIAMS (*aside*): Major Gordon, Hotel des Ambassadeurs. (*aloud*) This Major Gordon knows you, then?

ALBERT: By name only. He lived with his brother, Doctor Gordon, in the same province as me.

SIR WILLIAMS: But if this is all true, why then do you want to break up with Baccarat?

ALBERT: Because I can no longer go on deceiving her. I love another woman, a woman of whom I despair of being worthy. One has to be illustriously noble and very rich to pretend to the hand of Mademoiselle Concepcion de Sallandrera.

SIR WILLIAMS: It is Concepcion de Sallandrera whom you love?

ALBERT: Yes. Sir Williams, here's my letter for Baccarat.

SIR WILLIAMS: I will deliver it to her right away.

ALBERT: Thank you. On my return from Marseille, my first visit will be to you.

SIR WILLIAMS: When are you leaving Paris?

ALBERT: Tomorrow morning at 6 a.m. Goodbye and thank you again!

(*Albert leaves; Rocambole stealthily emerges from behind a curtain.*)

ROCAMBOLE: I say, my good Master, this doesn't bode good at all.
SIR WILLIAMS: You were there and heard everything?
ROCAMBOLE: I am moved to admit it. When I returned, I was first going to the salon, but when I walked through the library, which is separated from this room only by a curtain, I heard your voice and, truth to tell, what was being said interested me very much, so I stayed to listen.
SIR WILLIAMS: Your nobility and your millions may be a bit compromised, not to mention your future fiancée.
ROCAMBOLE: Yes, it does complicate matters somewhat.
SIR WILLIAMS: You think everything is ruined, right?
ROCAMBOLE: No!
SIR WILLIAMS: Ah ha! And what, according to you, must be done to fix the problem?
ROCAMBOLE: A bold stroke. Let's get rid of Monsieur Albert here and I'll go in his place to show that Major Gordon the portrait inside the medallion we'll have taken from him previously.
SIR WILLIAMS: Hum! Not bad! But how to get rid of Monsieur Albert discreetly and without arousing suspicions?
ROCAMBOLE: Baccarat is besotted with him. We could use her to bait a trap...
SIR WILLIAMS: Clever, that.

ROCAMBOLE: We need a safe place to do the deed. Do you have one in mind?

SIR WILLIAMS: Do you?

ROCAMBOLE: Yes.

SIR WILLIAMS: Bravo!

ROCAMBOLE: In Bougival. There's a small inn by the river in the middle of nowhere–The Red Inn, it's called. There's a little boat moored there for the customers who like to enjoy a tryst on the Isle de Croissy. We can lure Albert there...

SIR WILLIAMS: As luck would have it, if I recall correctly, it's precisely at the Isle de Croissy that Albert and Baccarat first met. It's the ideal location for a murder. Albert will go there, thinking he's going to meet Baccarat–Baccarat determined to kill herself. Yes, that should prove compelling enough.

ROCAMBOLE: A word of caution, my good Master. If you lure that woman to Croissy, she will get in our way.

SIR WILLIAMS: Leave Baccarat to me, Rocambole. Take my carriage, run to Bougival, get everything ready and wait for me.

ROCAMBOLE: See you soon then, Sir Williams.

SIR WILLIAMS: 'Till later, my dear Marquis.

ROCAMBOLE (*aside*): I made myself into Rocambole. You've made me a Marquis, my good Master. But no one, not even you, even if you were the Devil in person, will make me back into Joseph Fipart.

(*Rocambole leaves by the left. Fanny enters by the right.*)

FANNY (*to Sir Williams*): Tea is served, My Lord.

SIR WILLIAMS: Ah, you've arrived just in the nick of time, my dear. Listen, the time has come for you to prove your gratitude to me. When I leave here, go to the winter garden. Bring your mistress' hat with you.

FANNY: Why?

SIR WILLIAMS: It's not for you to know. And tell my coachman to get my coupé ready. We'll be leaving soon.

FANNY: "We?" Ah... I've promised to do as you ask...

SIR WILLIAMS: You have (*aside*) Money well spent.

(*Baccarat arrives by the right.*)

BACCARAT: Alone! You're alone! He's gone!

SIR WILLIAMS: Monsieur Albert has gone, true. There was nothing I could do to stop him...

BACCARAT (*tragic*): I knew it. He's gone.

SIR WILLIAMS: ...But he left me a letter for you.

BACCARAT: A letter? Why would he write a letter when he could just as well speak to me. Oh, this is terrible. May I have it?

SIR WILLIAMS: Why, you are trembling.

BACCARAT: I have a cold! Give it to me! (*reading*) He's leaving me. Leaving me forever. Oh! Surely you must know the reason. You're silent. Does he love another woman?

SIR WILLIAMS: He's getting married.

BACCARAT: Married! Albert? Who only days ago was weeping at my feet? Impossible!

SIR WILLIAMS: Yet, that's the truth.

BACCARAT: Ah! I will stop that marriage, at any cost.

SIR WILLIAMS: This may surprise you, but in this matter, you and I may share a common interest.

BACCARAT: We do?

SIR WILLIAMS: Yes. Let's say for argument's sake that I may be Monsieur Albert's rival...

BACCARAT: I see. You're jealous, too! In that case, we do indeed share a common purpose.

SIR WILLIAMS: I think so. Albert plans to leave Paris in the morning–to go and meet his future bride.

BACCARAT: How could he deceive me so? Do this to me? Doesn't he realize that his gesture will drive me insane?

(*She is about to leave when Sir Williams pulls her back.*)

SIR WILLIAMS: Wait. Don't go!

BACCARAT: I want to go and talk to him.

SIR WILLIAMS: Where?

BACCARAT: At his place.

SIR WILLIAMS: He's not there.

BACCARAT (*stubbornly*): I want to see him. I know that if I talk to him, he won't leave.

SIR WILLIAMS: I'm sure you're right, but you don't know where he is. Please, let me advise you in this.

BACCARAT: What do you suggest I do then? I'll do anything as long as I can get to talk to Albert one more time.

SIR WILLIAMS: You will. Write what I am going to dictate to you.

BACCARAT (*placing herself to write*): Go ahead. I'm ready.

SIR WILLIAMS (*dictating*): "Dearest Albert: I have read your letter. I do not plan to outlive your departure. Do you remember the Isle de Croissy? We met there for the first time and it was there that you told me that you loved me..."

BACCARAT: True!

SIR WILLIAMS: "...It's there that I intend to die. Tomorrow, the fishermen will find my corpse on its banks, the corpse of the woman you called your Baccarat."

BACCARAT (*writing feverishly*): And I will do just as I wrote.

SIR WILLIAMS: More likely, Albert will rush to the Isle–once the cradle of your love–to talk you out of killing yourself–I believe he still has feelings for you, after all–and you will have your opportunity. In just two hours, I'll have this note delivered to him. Then, allow me to escort you to Bougival.

BACCARAT: Of course. Here's the letter.

SIR WILLIAMS (*taking it and folding it*): Fine. I will return in two hours, but not before. Be patient, be calm. (*aside*) In two hours, it'll all be over.

(*Sir Williams leaves.*)

BACCARAT: Be patient! Be calm! How can I be calm when fever burns my insides, when I'm losing my mind. Oh! if Albert resists my prayers, my tears, I will kill myself before his eyes, in his arms! Yes, I will kill myself! Oh! My God! And all my guests are still here. (*ringing*) I'll tell Fanny to go say that I'm ill... Getting married! Him! Albert, who has neither family nor fortune. Then this woman must really love him. But, who is she? Oh! I want to know her; I want to fight her! Albert is my treasure, my life. (*ringing again*) Where the blazes is that girl? Fanny!

(*Baptiste enters.*)

BAPTISTE: Madame? You're still here?

BACCARAT: What do you mean? What are you doing here?

74

BAPTISTE: I would have bet that I just saw Madame leave in a coupé with the British Milord. I thought I recognized Madame's hat.

BACCARAT: I don't understand. What does this mean?

BAPTISTE (*remembering*): Ah, another thing, Madame That Russian Comte Artoff just left, but before he walked out, he wrote a few words on a piece of paper and told me to give it to you urgently.

BACCARAT: What do I care for Artoff and his love notes now! Leave it here and find Fanny. Where has that girl gone!

(*Baptiste leaves.*)

BACCARAT (*alone*): Artoff! I thought he had given up on me! (*reading*) "Dearest Lady: A chance conversation between my coachman and another driver has revealed to me that a trap has been set for Monsieur Albert tonight at Bougival. If he goes to the rendezvous you allegedly gave him, he is as good as dead. Since it's obvious you can't live without him, I hope you'll succeed in saving his life. Comte Artoff." My God! A trap–and it's I who unwittingly set it. I who will be responsible for his death! Oh, no!

(*Baptiste returns.*)

BAPTISTE: Madame! Fanny's not in her room.

BACCARAT: It all becomes clear now. She, too, is part of the conspiracy! Oh, the infamy–I must leave for Bougival right now. Have my carriage be readied at once!

(*She wraps herself in a cloak and takes a dagger.*)

BACCARAT: I will save Albert, and those who trapped me will pay dearly for it–or I will kill myself if I'm too late!

(*She walks out.*)

CURTAIN

Scene III

The Seine riverbank across from the Isle de Croissy. To the left are a few trees and a post to which is tied a small boat. To the right, occupying a good third of the stage, is the Red Inn. Its interior (which is visible) is miserably furnished with a table, a few chairs and an armoire; it includes a window and two doors, one opening onto the riverbank to the left and the other onto the road outside, to the right. A sign faces the public identifying the location. At the back of the stage, we see the river and the Isle.

Two couples enter left, followed by Maman Fipart.

JEAN GUIGNON: Well, Mademoiselle Cerise! What do you think of Bougival?

CERISE: It's quite enchanting: these trees, these flowers... What could be prettier?

ALPHONSE (*to Tulipe*): And is my lovely landlady having a good time, too?

TULIPE: I always have a good time in the country. I only wish Madame Fipart weren't so sad–

MAMAN FIPART: I didn't want to come–you insisted. And you see, my sadness is worse than your joy.

JEAN GUIGNON: Come on! I'm sure your scoundrel of a son will return eventually. Let's all have a drink in that inn. It'll cheer you up.

TULIPE: Here? Oh! my faith, no! It looks–villainous.

JEAN GUIGNON: Well, that one doesn't look very inviting, true, but there are others...

TULIPE: I'd rather do it at the restaurant where we lunched earlier.

(*They hear the music of boatmen in the distance.*)

JEAN GUIGNON: Ah! Boatmen are coming.
ALPHONSE: With an orchestra?
TULIPE: It's a holiday. Cerise, look! It's Agathe, Julie and our friends from the shop, with their brothers and cousins. What luck! Over here! Over here!
JEAN GUIGNON: Hey-o, the boat! Hey-o!
SHOUTS (*off*): Hey-o! Hey-o!
JEAN GUIGNON: This way–over here!

(*Several small boats arrive and a bunch of people get out, singing and playing instruments. The musicians stay at the back of the stage, near the river. Tulipe and Cerise embrace several boatgirls. Alphonse and Jean shake hands with some of the men.*)

JEAN GUIGNON: Ladies and gentlemen. Boatmen and Boatgirls! I'm very pleased to see you! You row magnificently. Now, I'd like to invite you to a dance, a *rondeau* composed by a friend of mine whose melodies are currently the toast of Paris.
ALL: Bravo!
JEAN GUIGNON: It's agreed, then? I'll start, but pay attention now: in the refrain, everyone must break something!
ALL: But, we don't have anything to break!
JEAN GUIGNON: True, true! Well, then, break–your voice! And sing loud! Now I begin:
There were once three boatgirls
And three boatmen all well dressed
Who one jolly day left from Asnières
To go see the country!

78

An old man of the crew
Stored their provisions
Which consisted of cheese
Three prunes and ten gherkins.
CRICK! CRACK!

CHORUS:

CRICK! CRACK! What a racket!
Hey-o-the boat!
Hold close to the helm
And sail on the water.

JEAN GUIGNON:

Without any incident
They sailed for two days
But then. lo, one started talking politics
And this got them fighting
They threw plates at each other
The ladies they knocked as well
Which proves that voyages
Are just an excuse for a good romp.
CRICK! CRACK!

CHORUS:

CRICK! CRACK! What a racket!
Hey-o-the boat!
Hold close to the helm
And sail on the water.

JEAN GUIGNON:

The saddest part of the story
Is that they got lost on the river
With nothing to eat or to drink
Not the least onion soup.
One of the ladies of the crew
Was eaten for dinner
She had on so much makeup

That everybody was poisoned
ALL: Bravo! Bravo!

(*They dance on the refrain. Night comes on.*)

ALPHONSE: I think it's time for supper.
JEAN GUIGNON: Well said! En route! And, on the way, let's play the music again. It'll amuse the fish.

(*They all embark aboard the boats and row away to the same tune.*

(*Then Rocambole appears, entering from the right into the Inn; he is dressed as a sailor.*)

ROCAMBOLE: Everything is ready. I'm alone, but at home here. I gave the owner of this dive 100 sous to go to the Batignolles for the night. He won't be back until morning. (*pulling out his watch*) In ten minutes, those I'm waiting for will arrive–let them come, I'm ready. I've got an idea that's quite ingenious. Sir Williams, won't be expecting the little surprise I've got in store for him. I really understood you, my good Master, you want to use me to pull your chestnuts from the fire, and then you'll get rid of me. But one doesn't fool Rocambole so easily. I found something else besides money in your desk... I know how to reach my goal now, and I won't have to share a fortune for it! Let's review my plan. Venture is likely to come, too. Sir Williams needs him in order to get our two birds onto the island. But I've worked him into my plan. I've rigged the boat and I know this river like a fish. I'm confident that...

(*Suddenly, the sounds of a carriage causes him to look at the window.*)

ROCAMBOLE: There they are... No! It's Sir Williams' coupé–and there he is. But who's this woman he's with? Could it be Baccarat?

(*Enter Sir Williams and Fanny, wearing Baccarat's hat.*)

FANNY (*looking around*): Oh, what a scary place!
ROCAMBOLE (*low to Sir Williams*): I'm here.
FANNY (*to Sir Williams*): Why did you bring me here?
SIR WILLIAMS: Not for a mere stroll in the moonlight, my dear. We must lure Monsieur Albert onto the Isle. For that, he must believe he's following Baccarat. That's why I've brought you here and made you wear her hat.
FANNY: All this to win a bet!
SIR WILLIAMS: Yes. A bet you will make me win–and the stakes will be for you.
FANNY: Go on, then–I can't resist you.
SIR WILLIAMS (*low to Rocambole*): I'm going to take a quick look outside then I'll hide. Get ready to take this girl to the Isle as soon as I spot Albert's arrival–Venture is bringing him here.
ROCAMBOLE: Will Venture be going on the boat with us, too?
SIR WILLIAMS: Yes.
ROCAMBOLE (*aside*): Perfect.
SIR WILLIAMS (*to Fanny*): Wait here, rest and count what's in this purse. I'm paying you in gold this time. (*to Rocambole*) The boat is just outside. Get ready to take her to the Isle, then come back.

(*He leaves by the door to the right.*)

ROCAMBOLE (*aside*): Excellent. He doesn't suspect a thing.

(*He, too, departs, but by the door leading to the riverbank.*)

FANNY (*alone, emptying her purse on the table*): Oh, such beautiful gold! There are nine coins! That's a lot.

(*Fanny counts them. At the same moment, the door giving onto the road outside opens. A woman, breathless, her clothes in disarray, enters. It is Baccarat.*)

BACCARAT: That was Sir Williams' coupé outside. They must be inside! (*seeing Fanny who has not noticed her*) And there's Fanny. (*loudly*) Girl!

(*Fanny sees Baccarat and rises in terror. Baccarat quickly locks both doors. She then strikes Fanny, pushes her down onto the table and shines her dagger's blade at her throat.*)

BACCARAT: Mustn't scream, mustn't budge–or I'll kill you.
FANNY: Mercy, mercy, mistress!
BACCARAT: There's no "mistress" here, foolish girl, only a desperate woman who's going to kill the bitch who betrayed her–if she doesn't tell her what she knows. Tell me about the trap set for the man I love and whom I'll save at any cost.
FANNY: I don't know anything.
BACCARAT: Then you die.

FANNY: No, no! He gave me money to take your hat and play make believe it was you going to Bougival. He. The Englishman. The man who was in the coach with me.

BACCARAT: Sir Williams?

FANNY: Yes.

BACCARAT: And where is he?

FANNY: Outside. Waiting for Monsieur Albert.

BACCARAT: To kill him, right?

FANNY: No, Madame! You're mistaken. It's only a bet. Sir Williams brought me here, hoping that, in the darkness and with the help of your hat, Monsieur Albert will mistake me for you. Out there, on the riverbank, there's a boat ready. When they see Monsieur Albert's carriage come, they'll call me. I'll get in the boat and they'll carry me across the Seine to the Isle de Croissy. Then, Monsieur Albert, spying you on the Isle, will want to cross the river, too. And this way, Sir Williams will win his bet.

BACCARAT: Come on, get up! You're being deceived, my poor girl. It's to murder him that they are luring Monsieur Albert here, not for a bet

FANNY: Mercy! And what are you going to do?

BACCARAT: I'll take your place. Come on! Quick, give me my hat!

FANNY: Here it is! Oh! You will forgive me?

BACCARAT: Yes, but only if I save Albert. (*suspicious*) But in asking for mercy, perhaps you're already thinking of new ways of betraying me–

FANNY: Me! Oh no, I swear–

(*There's knocking at the door leading to the right.*)

SIR WILLIAMS (*outside*): Here's our man!

(*Then, there is knocking at the door on the riverbank side.*)

ROCAMBOLE (*outside*): The boat is ready. Come quickly!
BACCARAT: They mustn't see this girl here. Ah, this armoire. (*She runs to the armoire and opens it*) Ah! There! Hide yourself in there! Do as I say, or else–

(*Baccarat forces Fanny to go inside the armoire and locks it. She then puts out the light and goes to open the door behind which Rocambole stands.*)

ROCAMBOLE: Come on! Come on! Let's embark–and faster!

(*Baccarat follows Rocambole on the riverbank. They step inside the boat moored there. Rocambole unties the boat and starts rowing away.*)

CURTAIN

Scene IV

The shores of the Isle de Croissy; the stage is raised and decorated with trees and willows. One tier is lower, filled with water, representing the river Seine. At the rear, one can see the village of Chaton and a few lit houses.

BACCARAT (*looking*): The boat that brought me here has returned to the other side. Ah! Albert has just arrived. He stands on the shore. He's seen me! He's embarking. But there are two other men with him... Who are they? They're taking the oars from the man who took me across. He's standing at the helm. They're rowing... No... Why are they letting the boat be dragged by the current? Ah! Armand is standing up. He's ordering them to come straight to the island. The two rowers are getting up. The helmsman is rushing on Albert. Ah! A knife–I saw a knife flash! Albert's struggling–he's fighting. They're going to murder him.

(*We hear a scream, followed by a splash.*)

BACCARAT (*letting out a terrible scream*): Ah! They've killed him! They've killed him!

(*Baccarat falls in a faint behind a willow. At this moment, the rowboat appears, carrying Rocambole, Venture and Sir Williams.*)

SIR WILLIAMS: We've done it. Rocambole, are you sure that the river will take good care of disposing of the body?

ROCAMBOLE (*wrapping a handkerchief around his hand*): I'm sure of it. There's a whirlpool in these waters that has dragged many a swimmer to his death.

SIR WILLIAMS: You are wounded?

ROCAMBOLE: In the struggle with Armand, I cut my hand. It's nothing.

SIR WILLIAMS: All that remains for us to do is to go back to Paris–and take off for Marseille. Do you have the portrait?

ROCAMBOLE: I do, but all things considered, I think I'll be going to Marseille alone.

VENTURE (*at the rudder*): What?

SIR WILLIAMS: You wretch! You wouldn't dare!

ROCAMBOLE: I would–and I do.

(*Rocambole pulls a small pistol from his sleeve and fires at Sir Williams. Sir Williams screams, puts his hand to his face and slumps over.*)

VENTURE: Watch out! The boat's going to capsize! It's filling with water!

ROCAMBOLE: It may be because I rigged the boat, my friend–we're all going to take a bath!

VENTURE: I can't swim! Help! Hel–!

(*Rocambole places his hand over his mouth as the boat sinks. All three men disappear into the dark waters. Then, we see one man swimming. It is Rocambole. He reaches the shore and steps onto the bank.*)

ROCAMBOLE: There! Venture and my former master are now sleeping at the bottom of the Seine! I am the only Chamery and I don't have to share that fortune with anyone else. The accounting will be much simpler. Ah!

The Devil! I was forgetting that woman–what if, by chance, Fanny remained behind and saw something!

(*He pulls out a knife, but suddenly, in the distance, we hear the songs of the Boatmen.*)

ROCAMBOLE: Oh! Oh! Company! I don't like curious folk. Hit the road, Rocambole, hit the road.

(*The curtain falls as he vanishes into the night.*)

CURTAIN

ACT III

Scene V

The Hotel Sallandrera. A small room giving on the reception room of the hotel. Curtained doors at the back. Side doors and doors at the rear. Richly furnished.

TOMAS: I've done what you've asked. I've announced you to Mademoiselle Concepcion, but as I told you, there's a party this evening at the Hotel, and she won't see you now.

JEAN GUIGNON: And I tell you again that Mademoiselle Concepcion will be greatly pleased to see me–and especially to listen to me.

TOMAS: You?

JEAN GUIGNON: Yes, me! I don't have the ordinary luck other men have. The proof of it is that my marriage failed to take place. Still, it was lucky that one of the cleaners fell ill–lucky for me, not for him–and I was dispatched in his place. As I was cleaning Mademoiselle's painting studio, I discovered the portrait of a face with which I am intimately acquainted...

TOMAS: Here? A face with which you would be intimately acquainted?

JEAN GUIGNON: Very intimately, since that face is mine.

TOMAS: I don't believe you.

JEAN GUIGNON: You're wrong. What happened was that I once posed for a portrait of Ganeesh. Monsieur Albert found something of India in me and used me as his model. So, while I was admiring myself,

Mademoiselle Concepcion walked in. She, too, was struck by the resemblance, and was polite enough to tell me. I told her how I found myself in a Hindu temple. When she learned that I knew Monsieur Albert, who had been her teacher, she became interested in me right away. And this is why I'm certain that she will receive me very nicely. Wait, someone's coming. I bet it's her.
TOMAS: My word, he's right. It's the young mistress.

(*Concepcion enters.*)

CONCEPCION: I'm very happy to see you, my friend.
JEAN GUIGNON (*aside to Tomas*): What did I tell you?
CONCEPCION: Leave us, Tomas.
JEAN GUIGNON: Yes, leave us, my good man.
TOMAS (*aside*): What is it that Mademoiselle can have to say to a floor sweeper?
JEAN GUIGNON: If your mistress needs you, I'm sure she'll call you. Go!

(*Tomas leaves.*)

CONCEPCION (*excitedly*): Are you bringing me news?
JEAN GUIGNON: Yes, Mademoiselle.
CONCEPCION: At last!
JEAN GUIGNON: After Monsieur Albert suddenly left his little house in Belleville two months ago, we heard nothing from him. This worried us all; even Mademoiselle Tulipe, our landlady, began to fear for her rent. Yesterday, an unknown gentleman appeared on behalf of Monsieur Albert, took away his paintings–after having paid the rent, of course–and the only thing he said to us was that Monsieur Albert had left Paris and that he would never return.

CONCEPCION (*aside*): He left without seeing me, without saying a word of goodbye to me.

JEAN GUIGNON: I thought this would be of interest to Mademoiselle, because I knew that she, too, was worried over Monsieur Albert.

CONCEPCION: You were right. I thank you for coming here to tell me. I want to reward your initiative.

JEAN GUIGNON: Oh, Mademoiselle, I didn't race here from Belleville to the Faubourg Saint-Germain for money. Your gratitude is enough reward for my trouble. Still, since Mademoiselle is so good, may I ask her for a favor–not for me, but for two other persons. I've told Mademoiselle that I was planning to marry Mademoiselle Cerise, Maman Fipart's niece, and that I reside with her aunt in the same house as Monsieur Albert. Well, these two are good, saintly women, Mademoiselle! Imagine that, by their skill at needlework, they had managed to accumulate enough money to pay the debts of Maman Fipart's son, a nasty character who's left for America–God be thanked! The worthy woman used all of her savings–she has none left. Moreover, Mademoiselle Cerise has now fallen ill and Maman Fipart spends her days and nights caring for her. Then, no work, and in the world of the poor, no work means no money...

CONCEPCION: I understand. I will be pleased to help these poor women. Here, take these gold coins to them right away.

JEAN GUIGNON: Excuse me, Mademoiselle, but I'm not asking for charity–they wouldn't accept it. It's work that they need; they are seamstresses, the best, skilled as fairies. I've learned from your concierge that there may be some work here that could be given to them; it's for that work that I am asking you, on their behalf.

CONCEPCION: Oh! Of course! We'll find some today, right now! We mustn't make that poor woman wait. Bring her to me this very evening. Will she accept an advance on her work?

JEAN GUIGNON: On her work? Oh! yes, indeed, that's different.

CONCEPCION: What's her name already?

JEAN GUIGNON: Maman Fipart.

(*Concepcion rings and Tomas returns.*)

CONCEPCION (*to Tomas*): A woman named Maman Fipart will come here this evening and ask to see me; you will let her in immediately and inform me of her arrival.

TOMAS: Yes, Mademoiselle. His Highness the Duke asks if Mademoiselle will see him?

CONCEPCION: My father? Of course!

JEAN GUIGNON: Ah, Mademoiselle, to be rich and charitable like you is to do a bit of God's work on Earth. I will bring Maman Fipart this evening. Goodbye! And all my thanks!

(*Jean bows and leaves, followed by Tomas.*)

CONCEPCION (*alone*): Was I deceived? Did Albert truly love me?...

(*The Duke de Sallandrera enters.*)

DUKE: Good evening, my child. I'm not disturbing you?

CONCEPCION: Oh, father! Never!

DUKE: Concepcion, I've come to talk to you–and talk seriously–about the Marquis de Chamery. I've already told you of the interest I took in this young man. I've opened my house to him. I've admitted him into our home and now, I'd like him to become part of our family...

CONCEPCION: I don't understand you, father.

DUKE: The Marquis de Chamery is the one person I wanted to find before dying–to repair a fatal error–to fulfill a solemn promise I made to a dying man. I neither can, nor ought to, say more. Concepcion; know only that your father is counting on you to accomplish a sacred duty–and in that, I am certain of your obedience.

CONCEPCION: Yes, father, but what am I to do?

DUKE: My dear child, you must consent to become Marquise of Chamery.

CONCEPCION: Marry him? But I don't love him, father!

DUKE: Listen to me carefully, child. If it was a question of saving my life by contracting this marriage, would you hesitate?

CONCEPCION: Oh! You know quite well I would give up everything for you!

DUKE: Well, my dear child, it's more than my life you are going to repurchase, it's my honor as a gentleman. I've given my word, and the one who received it can no longer release me from it for between us, now, there's only the marble of the tomb.

CONCEPCION (*weeping*): Oh, father, father! You are demanding my unhappiness.

DUKE (*softly*): Your unhappiness! Why? Your heart is free. The Marquis is young, rich, noble! He loves you and you will love him, too, when you get to know him better.

CONCEPCION: Love him?

(*Tomas returns.*)

TOMAS: The Marquis de Chamery solicits the honor of being received by His Highness.
CONCEPCION: Ah! He is here already.
DUKE: He's here to learn of your response. (*to Tomas*) Show him in. (*to Concepcion*) Remember, Concepcion, that it's your fiancé who's about to enter.
CONCEPCION: I will, father.
DUKE: Very good, child.
CONCEPCION (*aside*): Ah! Albert! Albert!

(*Rocambole enters as Tomas leaves.*)

ROCAMBOLE: Your Highness! Mademoiselle! Please excuse my impatience. But I could not resist the impulse of coming here...
CONCEPCION: Monsieur, the reply that you ask of me, my father has already conveyed to you.
DUKE: My dear Marquis, we are prepared to sign the contract of marriage this evening.
ROCAMBOLE: Oh, Mademoiselle, how can I express–
CONCEPCION: My father alone is entitled to your thanks, Monsieur. He orders and I obey.

(*Tomas returns.*)

TOMAS: Your Highness, the notary has arrived.
DUKE: Ah, yes. Show him into my office. (*to Rocambole*) My dear Marquis, please allow me to leave to draw up the major clauses of our contract.

CONCEPCION: If you are expecting company, father, I think I will retire now.

DUKE: That's fine. I'll walk you to your rooms. (*to Rocambole*) Till later, my friend–my son!

ROCAMBOLE (*seeking to kiss Concepcion's hand*): Mademoiselle, will you allow me–

CONCEPCION (*withdrawing her hand quickly and curtsying coldly*): Till later, Monsieur.

(*Concepcion leaves with her father and Tomas.*)

ROCAMBOLE (*alone*): The girl is cold! Bah! I will warm up this pretty statue. And if she remains of stone, she will at least have a gold pedestal. I know now the extent of the Sallandrera fortune. With my five millions, I am but a beggar compared to this Spanish grandee. Ah! If my poor master were still in this world, he would see that the affair was even more lucrative than he supposed. After that little scuffle in Bougival, everything went along just fine. I presented myself at the Hotel des Ambassadeurs in Marseille. There, I found Major Gordon, who had been instructed by the late Marquis de Chamery to locate his legitimate heir. I showed him the famous portrait, and right there and then, the worthy Major wrote me an affidavit which, combined with the other documents I took from Sir Williams' home, make me, without questions, the new, legitimate Marquis de Chamery. I've gotten my inheritance and now, this very evening, the Duke de Sallandrera will give me his daughter's hand in marriage. His daughter! To me, who was once Joseph Fipart! Rocambole! And the best thing is, I don't have to pay or share this with anyone. All my former accomplices are gone. Only Fanny worried me a bit at first, but she had the bright idea of returning to

Chatou. So she saw nothing and can't say anything. I didn't know how easy it would be to become a Marquis and a millionaire...

(*Tomas returns.*)

ROCAMBOLE: What is it?
TOMAS: There's a stranger who missed Monsieur le Marquis at his home and begs him to see him here.
ROCAMBOLE: Did he say his name?
TOMAS: He wrote it on a playing card with a pencil.
ROCAMBOLE: Give it to me. (*he reads:*) "Doctor Gordon." (*aside*) Another Gordon? The Devil if this one knew the real heir of Chamery!
TOMAS: The gentleman asked me to draw Monsieur le Marquis' attention to the playing card itself.
ROCAMBOLE (*turning it over*): A Jack of Hearts–
TOMAS: Should I show him in?
ROCAMBOLE (*perturbed*): Yes–yes.

(*Tomas leaves.*)

ROCAMBOLE: A Jack of Hearts. Could it be?... No! It can't be! Sir Williams and Venture are dead! Quite dead!

(*Tomas returns and announces:*)

TOMAS: Doctor Gordon!

(*A man enters; his face is badly disfigured and a black kerchief hides his right eye. It is, of course, Andrea a.k.a. Sir Williams.*)

95

ROCAMBOLE (*aside, scrutinizing the man's face*): I don't recognize this man.

ANDREA: I knew you would see me.

ROCAMBOLE: You are going to tell me your business, Monsieur?

ANDREA: Certainly, certainly. (*low, to Rocambole, in a different tone of voice*) When we're alone.

ROCAMBOLE (*aside*): That voice... I must be mad. That voice can't be *his*–for that's not *his* face. (*to Tomas*) Leave us and don't let anyone else in.

(*Tomas leaves. Andrea sits down, puts his hat on the table, crosses his legs and looks at Rocambole, laughing.*)

ANDREA: Hello, Rocambole.

ROCAMBOLE: You! It's you! My master!

ANDREA: You never believed in ghosts, right? Well, maybe you'll change your tune now. Yes, it's really me, my dear friend. Your confusion is understandable, for I have changed–not for the better, I agree. A pistol shot to the face has somewhat marred the harmony of my features, but it was not a bad thing because, thanks to you, I've become a new man. Gone, Andrea de Felipone, leader of the Jack of Hearts, gone Sir Williams, baronet, who had a few, minor peccadilloes on his record. Enter Doctor Gordon, innocent like a newborn child, who can show with impunity his new face throughout the capitals of Europe. Without that card which I see trembles in your hand, you yourself would not have recognized me. Ah, indeed! There you are, all pale and haggard. You're telling yourself "Andrea never forgives!" Well, in this case, you're mistaken. I have a fondness for you. One must learn to excuse youthful enthusiasm.

ROCAMBOLE: Kill me, but don't mock me.

ANDREA: Now, now. Sit beside me and let's chat like the good friends we used to be.

ROCAMBOLE: Oh! Heavens, don't play with me like a tiger with a lamb.

ANDREA: Fear is addling your wits. Relax! Which artist would seek to destroy his best work? For that is what you are, my own creation–my masterpiece. Sit down, I tell you! True, it gives me some pleasure to see you tremble. Ingrate! You haven't yet asked me how I was able to get out of the little scrape in which you left me.

ROCAMBOLE: Then, you are invulnerable?

ANDREA: And insubmersible, it seems. After having twisted in the watery abyss into which you had sunk our boat, the very force of the whirlpool brought me back to the surface. I was fished out by some singing boatmen who were very concerned about my health and who took me to the local hospital. I quickly came back to my senses. In the same room, in the bed adjoining mine, was a poor, delirious devil. See how things fall out! It was an acquaintance of ours. I will tell you about that strange and lucky meeting later. But first, my dear Rocambole, let me tell you that when one searches a desk, one must inventory all of its contents. You took from me the documents proving the existence of the Marquis de Chamery, but you neglected to take other papers which prove that you are merely Joseph Fipart. Now, there's a mistake which also must be attributed to youthful enthusiasm. You still have a lot to learn and I still intend to remain your teacher.

ROCAMBOLE: I see. The tiger now shows his claws.

ANDREA: No! Not at all! An old friend offers you his hand. If vengeance is the pleasure of the gods, interest is

97

the motive of men. Yes, I could ruin you to revenge myself, but I prefer to save you to enrich myself.

ROCAMBOLE: Ah! yes, I begin to understand. To deliver Rocambole to justice would risk compromising yourself. To serve the new Marquis de Chamery is, indeed, better for you–and you've come to apprise me of the price that I will have to pay for your "services."

ANDREA: Indeed. Now we understand each other. (*tendering a paper to him*) Sign your name to this–your real name–and I'll forgive you for your past mistakes.

ROCAMBOLE (*after reading it*): The Devil! You want the entire fortune of the de Chamerys?

ANDREA: In exchange for the much greater Sallandrera one, which I leave to you and you alone. Frankly, my generosity astonishes me.

ROCAMBOLE: You were right before. Fear was addling my wits. I needed time to reflect and reassess my position. Let me say this to you: I owe you a debt, I recognize it.

ANDREA: That's very nice of you.

ROCAMBOLE: But I will never sign this.

ANDREA: You will do so immediately.

ROCAMBOLE: I no longer need you and one doesn't pay so dearly for past services.

ANDREA: Oh! I know you will pay, my little Rocambole! We have not yet exchanged roles. I am still the master and you're still the student, and I will prove it to you. You are at my mercy just like when I held you breathless under my knee. I told you I had a chance meeting at the hospital. Do you know who with? Albert, the real Marquis de Chamery.

ROCAMBOLE: Albert!

ANDREA: Yes, Albert, plucked from the Seine in a desperate condition, who was, like me, transported to the hospital.

ROCAMBOLE: Albert isn't dead?

ANDREA: Not in the least! You are somewhat unlucky in crime. The folks you murder are doing fine. It was only poor Venture who remained down there. He's dead–let's not speak ill of him anymore. Albert, victim of a frightful delirium, could not give away evidence. I understood how important it was for me to secure such a vital hostage. So I claimed to be Doctor Gordon and, as soon as it became possible, I had Albert transferred to my old hotel, Rue Saint-Louis, the seat of the former Club of the Jack of Hearts. Now that he has somewhat recovered, he is full of gratitude for all the care that I've lavished on him. He thinks I'm the brother of Major Gordon, who's asked me to continue helping him find his family. Do you think that if, through my virtuous efforts, he becomes the Marquis of Chamery at last, he will haggle about the price of his gratitude? And what could even Rocambole do all alone against Albert and I?

ROCAMBOLE (*aside*): I'm truly trapped. (*aloud*) I'll sign.

ANDREA: Before you do so, listen. The documents which attest that you are in reality Joseph Fipart are sealed inside an envelope which I have left in the care of a trusted man. If I fail for one single day to return to the Rue Saint-Louis, this man has been instructed to deliver these documents to the Imperial Prosecutor. You understand what I'm saying?

ROCAMBOLE: I do. I will pay your price. (*aside*) As if I had a choice. (*aloud*) But in exchange, you will deliver Albert to me?

ANDREA: I will do more than that. For that poor, befuddled Albert isn't your worst enemy.

ROCAMBOLE: He isn't? Who else, then, do I have to worry about now?

ANDREA: There was a woman at the Isle de Croissy who witnessed everything.

ROCAMBOLE: Fanny?

ANDREA: Fanny saw nothing. Fanny left Paris. Fanny is out of the picture. For it wasn't Fanny that you carried across the Seine to the Isle.

ROCAMBOLE: Who then?

ANDREA: It was Baccarat. You didn't see her, but she saw you.

ROCAMBOLE: How do you know that?

ANDREA: I have my sources. I know that the beautiful Baccarat, certain of her lover's death, thinks she knows his murderer and seeks him everywhere. She's a formidable enemy. She will give you neither grace nor mercy.

ROCAMBOLE: Pah! A girl who so easily forgot the living will soon forget the dead.

ANDREA: You don't know her as I do, Rocambole! She feels she was the unwitting cause of her Albert's death, so now she has only two goals: revenge and expiation. She's broken up with her friends, sold her horses, her carriages, her hotel. She's amassed quite a fortune. which she's divided into two halves: one to help the poor–that's expiation–the other to track down Albert's assassin–that's revenge. Baccarat now lives in a small, isolated house in Rue Saint-Maur. She's gone back to using her real name and calls herself Louise Charmet.

ROCAMBOLE: Louise Charmet...

ANDREA: In the end, the Devil has become an Angel, it seems. But, trust me, the Devil will return quickly if someone points to you and tells her: "This is the man you're seeking."

ROCAMBOLE: What can a single woman do against two men like us?

ANDREA: Heh! If that woman is Baccarat, I would wager plenty.

ROCAMBOLE: She only saw me once–at night.

ANDREA: That's enough to never forget you.

ROCAMBOLE: The Marquis de Chamery so much resembles me?

ANDREA: We shall both rest easier when Baccarat can no longer be an obstacle on our path, when we've shut her accusing eyes, choked off her vengeful voice. I've already arranged something. We will speak of it this evening.

ROCAMBOLE: But this evening, I'm signing my marriage contract.

ANDREA: Precisely! And could you have any other witness but your old, trusted friend, Doctor Gordon?

(*Tomas returns.*)

TOMAS: His Highness the Duke entreats the Marquis de Chamery to come to his office.

ANDREA: Excellent. You will introduce me to the Duke de Sallandrera as a renowned alienist who recently arrived from India, where you knew me very well.

ROCAMBOLE: So be it! Come along then. (*aside*) Here I am, back to being shackled on his chain; but I have good teeth. I will gnaw through it.

ANDREA (*taking his hat, aside*): You may have won the first round at Bougival, Rocambole, but I swear, I will win the last. (*aloud*) Come along. We're going to be like two inseparable friends again.

(*They leave.*)

Tomas (*to himself*): I've just told Mademoiselle there's someone else asking for her. Someone quite stunning.

(*Concepcion enters from the left.*)

CONCEPCION: Tomas, Who is that woman who wants to speak to me? Is she Monsieur Jean's seamstress? An old woman?
TOMAS: No, Mademoiselle. She's a beautiful lady, very beautiful.
CONCEPCION: Show her in! It's probably one of the ladies from our charity committee.
TOMAS (*announcing*): Madame Louise Charmet!

(*Baccarat enters, dressed in mourning. At a sign from Concepcion, Tomas leaves.*)

CONCEPCION: Will you please have a seat, Madame?
BACCARAT: Mademoiselle de Sallandrera, I am but a stranger to you. Yet I have come to solicit a favor from you, a grace.
CONCEPCION: Speak, Madame. Believe me when I say that I only desire to be agreeable to you.
BACCARAT: You are good and charitable, Mademoiselle. Your reputation as a good angel to the poor is well known. Through your charitable efforts, a lottery has been organized to benefit the homeless and a collection of prize paintings is being exhibited in this very Hotel. Chance led me to see it.

CONCEPCION: And you propose to offer me some *objet d'art* to enrich the collection?

BACCARAT: On the contrary, Mademoiselle. I've come to entreat you to give to me, at whatever price it pleases you to set, one of the prizes on display.

CONCEPCION: The poor will indeed benefit from your generosity.

BACCARAT: So you do consent?

CONCEPCION: Of course. Which painting is it?

BACCARAT: It's not a painting, only of a sketch, signed in the name of virtually an unknown artist, which can, perhaps, have value only for me.

CONCEPCION: There's only one sketch in our exposition–it was donated by Monsieur Albert.

BACCARAT: That's correct, Mademoiselle. I'm offering you 1,000 francs for that sketch.

CONCEPCION: I wouldn't have asked you for half that sum. In the name of the poor, I thank you, Madame.

BACCARAT: This sketch is a treasure for me. It's the memory of a lost past. Poor Albert. I can still see him drawing it at my home. It may have been his last work.

CONCEPCION: His last work! Has Monsieur Albert given up painting? Is it for that reason that he's stopped coming here to give me lessons these last two months?

BACCARAT: You will never see him anymore, Mademoiselle.

CONCEPCION: He went away?

BACCARAT: He's dead.

CONCEPCION: Dead? Albert! Oh! no! No, you're mistaken, Madame. Today, just now, I had news from him.

BACCARAT: That's impossible

CONCEPCION: A stranger went to his house, paid his rent and said that he'd had left Paris, never to return.

BACCARAT: Who told you this?

CONCEPCION: A honest lad named Jean who lives in the same house.

BACCARAT: That stranger must be one of the murderer's accomplices.

CONCEPCION: Murderer?

BACCARAT: Yes, Mademoiselle. Albert was murdered before my very eyes two months ago at the Isle de Croissy. He is dead.

CONCEPCION: Dead! And I was accusing him! Oh! I knew quite well that he couldn't have forgotten me. Poor Albert! And my heart never guessed and never told me, "weep and pray, wretched woman! Your love is dead." (*sobbing*) Dead! Oh, My God! My God!

BACCARAT: These tears! This despair! So, it was you whom he loved, Mademoiselle...

CONCEPCION: I loved him, too, Madame. Why hide it now? My love hurts no one.

BACCARAT (*aside*): It was for her that he left me. His last thoughts were for her.

CONCEPCION: You're weeping, too, Madame.

BACCARAT: It's not only tears that we each owe to our dearly departed. If you truly loved him, Mademoiselle, you will help me to avenge him, help me to find and punish his assassin.

CONCEPCION: Yes! Yes! I can do very little myself, but my father and the Marquis de Chamery can do much.

(*She rings; Tomas enters.*)

CONCEPCION: Beg Monsieur de Chamery to come find me here.

(*Tomas leaves.*)

BACCARAT: Who is this Marquis de Chamery?

CONCEPCION: He's my fiancé, Madame.

BACCARAT: Your fiancé? You loved Albert, but you're going to marry another man?

CONCEPCION: If I were mistress of my fate, not being Armand's betrothed, I would have been God's–but my father has contracted a debt of honor that I must repay at the cost of my happiness.

BACCARAT: Allow me to write a note, Mademoiselle.

CONCEPCION: To whom?

BACCARAT: To that lad, Jean, who lived with Albert. He saw that stranger; he will be able to give us his description, put us on his tracks. I'm going to ask him to come to my place this evening.

CONCEPCION: Good idea.

(*Baccarat starts writing. Completely occupied by what she is doing, she doesn't notice Rocambole who enters.*)

ROCAMBOLE: Mademoiselle, you called me and I rushed.

CONCEPCION: I have a service to ask of you, Monsieur.

ROCAMBOLE: Speak, Mademoiselle, and all that is in my power to do, I will do. What is it that you wish?

CONCEPCION: A young man in whom my father and myself were interested has disappeared. I've just learned that he was murdered two months ago at the Isle de Croissy.

ROCAMBOLE (*aside*): What!

CONCEPCION: Until now, the murderer has managed to escape justice, but that crime cannot remain unpunished any longer. I want you to help us discover his identity.

ROCAMBOLE (*aside*): She certainly knows a lot. (*aloud*) Who told you this?

CONCEPCION: A lady friend of Monsieur Albert, the victim. A witness to the crime.

ROCAMBOLE (*aside*): The Devil! (*aloud*) And this person?

BACCARAT: It is I, Monsieur.

(*Baccarat stands up but Concepcion is hiding Rocambole from her, placed as she is between the two of them.*)

CONCEPCION: This is Madame Charmet.

ROCAMBOLE (*aside*): Baccarat!

CONCEPCION: Marquis, you will lend us your support, your name, your credit. Please tell Madame Charmet that she can count on you.

ROCAMBOLE (*aside*): Danger looms ahead. No point in avoiding it. Let's face it boldly. (*walking to Baccarat and introducing himself face to face*) Madame, I am, I swear, completely at your service.

BACCARAT (*bowing*): Monsieur, I– (*she raises her head and sees Rocambole for the first time*) My God.

CONCEPCION: What's wrong?

ROCAMBOLE (*aside*): She's recognized me–only the most brazen audacity can now save me. (*aloud*) You were, you say, a witness to the murder of this unfortunate young man. Did you see the murderer close enough to be able to recognize him?

BACCARAT (*who hasn't taken her eyes off him*): Yes, yes, I did. (*aside*) The same features, the same look.

ROCAMBOLE (*with extraordinary assurance*): I see that you are indeed upset at reliving these somber moments, Madame Charmet. Still, to be useful to you, I need to know everything you saw.

CONCEPCION: The Marquis is right.

BACCARAT (*aside*): Is this a dream–a nightmare. (*low to Concepcion*) Who exactly is this young man?

CONCEPCION: The Marquis de Chamery–my fiancé.

ROCAMBOLE (*aside*): She doubts now.

BACCARAT (*aside*): It can't be him. And yet, his look freezes my heart. If he were to take off his gloves, I think I would still see the blood on his hands.

ROCAMBOLE: Get hold of yourself, Madame; sit down, I beg you. In any event, I repeat to you, I'm entirely at your service. Tell me, what clues do you have? What trail can I follow? What did the murderer look like? Was he young or old?

BACCARAT (*faintly*): Young.

ROCAMBOLE: Blonde or dark-haired?

BACCARAT: Dark-haired.

ROCAMBOLE: Why didn't you call for help, Madame? Perhaps someone would have come. Or did you fear you would share the same fate as Monsieur Albert?

BACCARAT: I wouldn't have hesitated to sacrifice my life to save his. But when I saw the blade of the knife disappear into his heart, I screamed. Then, I collapsed as if the same blow had struck me.

ROCAMBOLE: Then you only saw the features of the murderer incompletely? From a distance?

BACCARAT: No. I saw him–as I see you, Monsieur.

ROCAMBOLE: Truly? That's very lucky, that.

BACCARAT: I fainted behind some bushes. The cold of the night revived me and, when I opened my eyes, I saw shining near me the blade of a bloody knife, which the murderer was still holding. He had heard my scream and was now looking for me, trying to kill me. "If I die here," I thought then, "who will avenge Albert?" I remained motionless and silent. The murderer passed so close to me that his foot treaded on my dress–but he walked by without seeing me.

ROCAMBOLE (*aside*): Clumsy!

BACCARAT: When he disappeared in the woods, when the sound of his steps had gone, I got up. Then, in the fold of my dress, I found an object that the murderer had dropped.

ROCAMBOLE (*aside*): What?

CONCEPCION: What was it?

BACCARAT: A silver medallion with a lock of hair inside. Its chain must have caught on a branch and broke.

ROCAMBOLE: The Devil! My father's medallion!

BACCARAT: If God saved me miraculously from death, if he put this evidence in my hands, it's because He wants me to fulfill my mission, to find and punish Albert's assassin. Wherever he may be, I will find him, and be he strong, powerful or rich, I will destroy him!

ROCAMBOLE (*aside*): That's what we shall see. (*aloud*) The Duke de Sallandrera and I will assist you to the utmost, my dear Madame. From this day onward, your cause has become my cause.

CONCEPCION: *Thank* you, Marquis–

BACCARAT (*aside*): Ah! I must be mistaken.

(*Tomas returns.*)

CONCEPCION (*to the valet*): What do you want, Tomas?

TOMAS (*low to Concepcion*): I beg your pardon, Mademoiselle, but there's an old woman who is asking to see you. She says she's coming on behalf of Monsieur Jean.
CONCEPCION (*low*): Fine! Show her in.

(*Tomas leaves.*)

CONCEPCION (*to Baccarat, who looks like she's preparing to leave*): You are leaving, Madame?
BACCARAT: I'm expected at home.
CONCEPCION: I will take you to the gallery to pick up Albert's sketch and we will speak more about the one whom we both mourn.
ROCAMBOLE (*to Baccarat*): Madame, when can I have the honor of presenting myself at your home?
BACCARAT: Tomorrow, if you'd like.
ROCAMBOLE: Excuse me, but you haven't said–
BACCARAT: Where I live? No. 47, Rue Saint-Maur.

(*The two women leave.*)

ROCAMBOLE: I've managed to deflect that storm, but only for a day at most. Between my former master and Baccarat, I'm trapped as in a vice. I bought one off. I must be rid of the other. She can destroy me with that medallion. She's got her hands on my throat. Rocambole, my boy, you thought you'd reached safe harbor, when in fact, you've achieved nothing. I've got to do it all over again.

(*Tomas returns with Maman Fipart.*)

TOMAS: You may wait here for Mademoiselle de Sallandrera, my good woman.

(*He leaves. Maman Fipart at once recognizes her son.*)

MAMAN FIPART: Ah! Heavens! Joseph!

ROCAMBOLE (*aside*): My mother! Now, there's a meeting I wasn't expecting.

MAMAN FIPART: My son!

ROCAMBOLE (*aside*): No way I can fool this one.

MAMAN FIPART: Why aren't you answering me? It's really you, isn't it?

ROCAMBOLE: Well, yes, it's really me. Hello, mama.

MAMAN FIPART: Joseph! My child! In seeing you again, I'm forgetting my misery, your abandonment. I'm happy. Oh! yes, really happy.

ROCAMBOLE: Look, look, mama, calm down, no tears, especially no uproar. You're happy to see me again. That's understood.

MAMAN FIPART: How long have you been back? Why haven't you found time to come embrace your old mother?

ROCAMBOLE: Good Lord! I was thinking about it this very morning. I will tell you my business later, at your place. But you can't stay here. We mustn't be seen together.

MAMAN FIPART: Why's that?

ROCAMBOLE: I will tell you tomorrow–in Belleville.

MAMAN FIPART: Tell me at least how it is I find you in this posh Hotel dressed in these fine clothes?

ROCAMBOLE: I will tell you everything tomorrow. Hug me once, twice if you wish, and let me escort you to a carriage that will take you home. Well, why aren't you coming?

110

MAMAN FIPART: Joseph, now that the first moment of joy is passed, I'm afraid.

ROCAMBOLE: Afraid? Of what?

MAMAN FIPART: Of all these mysteries, of your presence here, in clothes that are not your normal clothes. Joseph, I know you. You're planning some evil deed.

ROCAMBOLE: Why, not at all! I'm shocked to hear you say this! I dress like this every day now. There's no mystery to it; I left to make my fortune. Once rich, I came back–that's all.

MAMAN FIPART: Rich in so short a time?

ROCAMBOLE: I was lucky. There'll be money in it for you, little mother, a good, fat income.

MAMAN FIPART: But how did you get rich?

ROCAMBOLE: I can't believe how curious you are! Well, since you must know, I speculated on sugar cane. There. Are you satisfied? I will explain tomorrow why it's necessary that no one must know that I'm Joseph Fipart. It could hurt my business. Surely, you wouldn't do anything to harm your little Joseph, who loves you dearly and will give you much money? Now let me escort you out of here quickly.

MAMAN FIPART: You would renounce your father's name? You're afraid someone will discover that I raised you? Joseph, you've often deceived me in the past, you've lied to me, but this time, you will tell me the truth. You will tell it to me right now, and I shan't leave until then.

ROCAMBOLE: You can't stay! You mustn't!

MAMAN FIPART: I will stay, I tell you! We'll see if you dare drive your mother out.

ROCAMBOLE: Hush! Someone's coming–

(*Tomas enters.*)

TOMAS (*to Maman Fipart*): Mademoiselle de Sallandrera can't see you now; she begs you to excuse her and to return tomorrow. (*to Rocambole*) His Highness the Duke is awaiting the Marquis de Chamery in the salon. The guests have begun to arrive.
ROCAMBOLE (*to Tomas*): Fine. I'll be there shortly. Go away.

(*Tomas starts to leave, but Maman Fipart holds him back.*)

MAMAN FIPART: Did you call him–the Marquis de Chamery?
TOMAS: Yes. This gentleman is the Marquis de Chamery, fiancéd to Mademoiselle de Sallandrera.
ROCAMBOLE (*pushing Tomas out*): Will you go now!

(*Tomas leaves.*)

MAMAN FIPART: So you're the Marquis de Chamery now! From whom have you stolen that name? Answer!
ROCAMBOLE: I told you before that tomorrow, you would know everything–tomorrow only.
MAMAN FIPART: And I intend to know today! I may be poor and miserable, but I'm honest. I don't want my son to commit an infamy.
ROCAMBOLE: Ah! Speak much lower. They might hear us!
MAMAN FIPART: Where will the ill be if they hear us? Where will the ill be if we disabuse those you intend to deceive?

ROCAMBOLE: I will tell you since you insist! The ill will be, quite simply, that they will send your son to the galleys. You've got it now?

MAMAN FIPART (*hiding her head in her hands*): Ah!

ROCAMBOLE: So are you going to keep quiet now? And do as I say?

MAMAN FIPART (*bursting into tears*): Oh, wretch! Wretch! But perhaps there's still time to save yourselves. Joseph! Listen to me! Give up this title! Give up this name! Tell me you'll do it! Spare my old age the shame and despair. (*kneeling*) Joseph, my child, I'm begging you on my knees...

ROCAMBOLE: Come on, mama, you're not being reasonable. I'll give up nothing.

MAMAN FIPART (*standing up*): Ah! I am cursed! Well, since my prayers and my tears are useless, since you have no decency in your heart, what your father would have done, I will do.

ROCAMBOLE: What do you mean?

MAMAN FIPART: I mean that I'm going to turn you in.

ROCAMBOLE: Come on now! A mother doesn't turn in her own son.

MAMAN FIPART: For me to be silent now would make me your accomplice. No, no. I have to speak up. I will say to those who are here: "This young man is my son and I'm his mother! And he's also a forger and a thief."

ROCAMBOLE (*threatening*): Take care, woman!

MAMAN FIPART: Oh! The only villainy left would be for you to raise your hand against your mother!

ROCAMBOLE: Me! Why, you know that I love you too much!

MAMAN FIPART: Kill me if you will. Death is preferable to dishonor.

ROCAMBOLE: Your melodrama is going to attract attention and you're going to destroy me.

MAMAN FIPART: You did it to yourself.

ROCAMBOLE: Someone's coming. Very well. Turn me in then.

(*Concepcion and the Duke of Sallandrera enter.*)

DUKE: What's going on here?

ROCAMBOLE (*low to Maman Fipart*): Say one word now and you will send me to the galleys.

MAMAN FIPART: Ah.

DUKE: Who is this woman?

ROCAMBOLE: I don't know her.

MAMAN FIPART (*aside, with infinite sadness*): He doesn't know me.

ROCAMBOLE: The dear woman fell prey, for some reasons that I don't know, to a nervous outburst. I was trying to calm her when you arrived.

DUKE: Madame, do you know the Marquis de Chamery?

MAMAN FIPART: The Marquis de Chamery, is he? (*she is going to speak*) Well, Monsieur– (*she sees Rocambole's look and stops*) No, I don't know this man. I didn't want to leave this house; it seems to me that God himself had led me here to save someone. But now–now, I want to leave, to leave right away–for if I stay, I will speak–and I cannot, my God, I cannot. (*falling into a faint.*)

CONCEPCION (*running to her*): Oh–get help, father. A doctor, quick, a doctor.

DUKE: Let's call Doctor Gordon.

CONCEPCION: Poor woman! The privations, the misery–

DUKE: So, you know her?
CONCEPCION: I've heard of her. She's a seamstress called Maman Fipart.

(*Doctor Gordon–Andrea–enters.*)

ANDREA (*aside*): Maman Fipart!
ROCAMBOLE (*to Andrea, low*): Yes, my mother.
ANDREA: Here! Did she say anything?
ROCAMBOLE: No, but she'll talk.
CONCEPCION: Help her, doctor.
ANDREA: Don't worry, Mademoiselle. It's only her nerves. I have on me just what's required to calm her. Here, my good woman, breathe this. I insist. It's necessary. (*presents a flask*) There! Again. That's fine.

(*Maman Fipart, who was struggling, falls back into the armchair to which she has been carried.*)

ROCAMBOLE: How pale she is!
CONCEPCION: My God! She is like dead now.
ROCAMBOLE: Dead! (*low, grabbing Andrea's arm*) You haven't killed her?
ANDREA (*low*): No! But she won't speak except when I want it. (*aloud*) Yet, one more time... Don't worry, Mademoiselle. Since you care for this woman, I'll take her home myself, in my carriage below.
ROCAMBOLE (*low*): Where will you take her?
ANDREA: To my place! I'll answer for her to you.
ROCAMBOLE: And I'll take care of Baccarat.

(*The Duke rings. Tomas and two valets enter.*)

CURTAIN

ACT IV

Scene VI

Baccarat's place. A small room modestly furnished. There is a door at the back, one on the left and a window on the right. AT RISE, Baccarat is alone, seated by a small round table, looking at a portrait attached to her neck by a gold chain. On the table, there is a candelabra with two branches with lamp shades.

BACCARAT: A portrait half effaced by my kisses and my tears. Here's all that remains to me of him–and the one whom he loved now prepares herself to marry someone else. Oh! She didn't love him the way I loved him–the way I will always love him!

(*She rings. An old servant enters.*)

BACCARAT: Antoine, did you go to the address I gave you?
ANTOINE: To Belleville? Yes, Madame. That Monsieur Jean had already gone out but I left your note.
BACCARAT: Good.
ANTOINE: Someone's just delivered a letter for you.
BACCARAT: Ah? Let's see it. As soon as Monsieur Jean arrives, bring him to me.
ANTOINE: Thérèse will do it, for I beg Madame to allow me to leave.
BACCARAT: Tonight?
ANTOINE: It's very urgent. It's a question of getting some money–Rue de l'Estrapade.

116

BACCARAT: Money?

ANTOINE: Which is falling out of the sky, seeing that I don't know why it's coming to me.

BACCARAT: Go, my friend. But tell Thérèse.

ANTOINE: Not to worry. I will also tell her to carefully lock all the doors.

(*Antoine leaves.*)

BACCARAT (*reading the letter*): "Doctor Gordon begs earnestly that Madame Charmet take the trouble of going this very evening to his Hotel, No. 3, Rue Saint-Louis, for some business of particular interest to Baccarat." "Doctor Gordon." I can't recall ever hearing that name. But there's nothing about Baccarat that is now of interest to Louise Charmet, so I won't go to this rendezvous. (*noise outside*) Antoine's leaving; they are locking the door. The Marquis de Chamery promised to come today, but it's getting late. I must no longer expect him. I really wanted to see him again, just to convince myself that his resemblance with the criminal I seek is only a trick of my imagination. In the moonlight, I was able to see the face of the murderer and the more I compare it with–but no, it's madness. The Marquis de Chamery didn't even know Albert. He wasn't even in Paris when the crime was committed. And what would be his motive? I repeat–it's madness... Nine o'clock. Monsieur Jean won't be home yet, so I won't see him until tomorrow. (*noise outside*) They're unlocking the gate. Someone's coming. I hear steps on the gravel in the garden. Is it Monsieur Jean. Why doesn't Thérèse come to announce him? She must still be there. (*goes to ring, the bell doesn't work*) The bell doesn't work. The wire must be broken for I rang Antoine earlier. (*calling*) Thérèse!

Thérèse! What? Am I alone? I'm sure I heard steps in the garden. Now I hear someone in there in the vestibule. That must be Thérèse.

(*Rocambole appears in the doorway.*)

ROCAMBOLE: No, Madame, it's me!

BACCARAT: Monsieur de Chamery.

ROCAMBOLE: Who found no one to announce him.

BACCARAT (*surprised*): No one?

ROCAMBOLE: The street door was open and I locked it behind me. I crossed your little garden, your vestibule and I didn't, I repeat to you, meet anyone.

BACCARAT (*to herself*): Thérèse cannot be far. (*aloud*) Be welcome, Marquis. I no longer expected your visit.

ROCAMBOLE: I'm coming a little late; but I swear to you that I've been thinking only of you since yesterday. (*taking off his hat*) You live in a rather isolated house. You're not afraid here?

BACCARAT: Afraid? What have I to be afraid of?

ROCAMBOLE: If the man you are pursuing with so much energy knew of your intentions towards him, if he knew you lived in an isolated house, and that you had only an old valet and young girl to defend you, why, that man might almost with impunity make a witness and her evidence disappear forever.

BACCARAT: I'm more than prepared to defend my life vigorously, were that the case, believe me. But please, sit down, I beg you.

ROCAMBOLE (*aside, going to take a seat*): No windows on the street–only one in the garden.

BACCARAT: You were saying that you have been thinking–

ROCAMBOLE: —About the affair that touches you so profoundly? Yes, Madame. I've already taken several steps, but I need more information. In particular, I need to see this evidence, this silver medallion that providence delivered into your hands.

BACCARAT: A medallion undoubtedly stolen by the wretch who wore it, for it's one of those they give as a reward to metal-workers for producing some particularly fine piece of work. It's been engraved with two initials that are still readable.

ROCAMBOLE: Would you be willing to show it to me?

BACCARAT: Of course.

(*She goes to a cupboard and opens it. Meanwhile, Rocambole shuts and locks the door to the neighboring room.*)

ROCAMBOLE (*aside*): I don't know where this door leads, so let's lock it. Once I have the medallion back, I will rid myself of this meddlesome woman.

(*Baccarat returns with a box that she places on the table near the light.*)

BACCARAT: Here it is. The medallion is inside this box, but it's a little difficult to open.

ROCAMBOLE (*removing the glove on his right hand*): Let me help you. (*advancing his hand, he tries to open the box; the light falls plainly on his hand*) There! It's open.

BACCARAT (*looking at his hand*): Ah!

(*She drops the box on the table; her glance remains fixed on Rocambole's hand.*)

119

ROCAMBOLE: What's the matter? What are you looking at? Ah! That scar? I was bitten by one of my dogs...

BACCARAT (*looking at the hand, then at Rocambole's face*): It is you. It's really you!

ROCAMBOLE: Come now, don't say silly things. Let me see that medal–

BACCARAT (*placing her hand on the box*): In his struggle with Albert, the murderer was wounded on his right hand. And you have a scar on your right hand. Ah, my memory didn't deceive me. My heart said it well. I've found the man I was looking for–and that man is you!

ROCAMBOLE: Me?

BACCARAT: Yes! You may be a rich nobleman, and what I am saying nay sound incredible, impossible even–but it is true. The Marquis de Chamery, the fiancé of Concepcion de Sallandrera is a murderer. Why did you kill Albert? I don't know. I don't understand it–yet. But kill him you did–and killed him like a coward. You came here, thinking by this excess of audacity, you would dispel my suspicions, triumph over my memories...

ROCAMBOLE: I thought you were a reasonable woman. Let's say that I'm the man you say. Should you be threatening me? Aren't you alone with me? Oh–quite alone! Your people won't be back for an hour. No one has seen me enter, no one will see me leave–and if a body is found here, in the midst of broken furniture, the Police will think you've fallen victim to a burglar. Come on, give me that medallion and we may still strike a bargain.

BACCARAT: Never!

ROCAMBOLE: Baccarat, I'm indeed, the man you saw on the Isle de Croissy, but if I confess now, it's because you are going to die.

BACCARAT: Die and leave you unpunished? God cannot want that. I will call for help. Someone will come.

ROCAMBOLE: Who? You have neither servants nor neighbors. No one uses this street. I couldn't have chosen a better location to get rid of you. Baccarat, we know each other too well. I know you wouldn't give me any mercy, and I won't show you any.

BACCARAT: To struggle seems impossible. You have taken your measures very carefully. I understand that you must reclaim this evidence at any cost, and to have it, you must kill me. Well, then, I will die by the same hand that struck my beloved Albert.

ROCAMBOLE: And this hand will strike you more surely than it struck him. (*pulling his dagger*) You won't have a Doctor Gordon to revive you.

BACCARAT: What? Albert is still alive?

ROCAMBOLE: Alas, yes. I missed him in Bougival, but I know where to find him, your Albert, and after you've been dealt with, I'll take care of him.

BACCARAT: Albert still lives and you're threatening him again, wretch! I'd have surrendered my life to you, but I'll fight for his. Yes, I must live to defend him! I will live, I will! I'm telling you this at the point of your knife. I'm a woman of the people! I'm used to violence; I have energy and courage. If I die here, Albert will be lost. Well, I don't intend to die!

(*She shoves Rocambole back.*)

ROCAMBOLE: Oh! you won't escape me this time.

(*He chases her around the room. Baccarat throws things at him, hides behind furniture, that Rocambole overturns as he pursues her. She screams and calls for help.*)

BACCARAT: My God! Protect me. A weapon, I need a weapon.

(*She knocks the chandelier over. The candles go out. The room is plunged in complete darkness.*)

ROCAMBOLE: If my eyes no longer perceive you, my hate will sense you.

(*He searches in the dark.*)

BACCARAT (*sliding along the wall*): He's locked all the doors but if I can reach the window, I'm saved.

(*She crawls towards the window.*)

ROCAMBOLE (*still searching*): I know she's here—somewhere.

(*Baccarat reaches the window and opens it; Rocambole hurls himself at her.*)

BACCARAT: The window!
ROCAMBOLE (*seizing her*): Ah! You're caught. Well caught.
BACCARAT (*screaming*): Help! Help! Murder!
ROCAMBOLE: Oh! I'll quickly stifle your voice.

(*A ray of moonlight illuminates the stage. We see Rocambole raising his right hand the one that holds the dagger. He is about to strike Baccarat, but she sees him and, using all her strength, she manages to get free from Rocambole's left hand, which was holding her.*

(*Instead of fleeing again, this time she rushes at Rocambole and, with her two hands, grasps his right and uses her better leverage to try to take away his dagger.*)

BACCARAT: Since I don't have a weapon, I will take yours.
ROCAMBOLE: Why, you demon!

(*Rocambole tries to free his hand, but Baccarat won't let go. She pushes it–and the dagger–down towards Rocambole's face; then, suddenly, she bites his hand hard.*)

ROCAMBOLE (*screaming*): Aarrr!
BACCARAT: You won't kill me, I'll save Albert! Help! Murder!

(*Knocking is heard at the door at the back.*)

BACCARAT: Ah! Someone's heard me! They're coming to my aid. Help! Break the door!

(*Someone breaks the door at the rear and enters–it is Jean Guignon. Baccarat utters a scream of joy, lets go of Rocambole and runs towards her savior.*

(*Rocambole escapes through the window.*)

BACCARAT: Ah, you have saved me!

JEAN GUIGNON: Saved you? Ah! Then, for once, I guess I've had some luck.

CURTAIN

Scene VII

A cellar that was once a counterfeiting factory. To the left and near the front of the stage are miscellaneous tools and an old, rusty printing press. Further back, we see a pile of crumbling stones that fell off a mossy wall eaten away by damp. In the back of the stage is a large, abandoned fireplace. To the right, through a stone arch, is a stone stairway consisting of six steps. An iron-wrought lamp illuminates this somber hovel. Rocambole is seated on the stone steps, his head between his hands, his clothes in disarray.

ROCAMBOLE: Baccarat beat me! I was forced to run like a rabbit. So I ran to Andrea's and I said: "Hide me– all is lost!" and he told me to wait here, in this hideaway in the bowels of his old Hotel. (*rising*) It's like a dungeon. But at least, here, I can pull myself together and think. Baccarat knows everything now; she's going to accuse me publicly; she has proof. My mother will talk, the poor woman, and the identity of Joseph Fipart will become known–it's all over. Come on, I won't try to struggle. I'll leave the Chamery title to whoever wants it and leave with the five millions that I had prudently withdrawn from the bank and hidden in my apartment. I have a lad who is devoted to me. I gave Andrea a note for him in which I instruct my servant to bring to me the safebox he'll find under the floor of my bedroom. There's five millions in it, and with it, Andrea and I can escape. Once in England, we'll share the loot–I can't do otherwise. Ah! I wish I hadn't tackled Baccarat! Or come here! I should have gone straight home, take my treasure, run to Boulogne and let Andrea wrap up this business by himself. But it's too late now. I lost my head; I only thought of finding a safe place to hide, and naturally, my first thought was to run to him. Andrea was as scared as I was, at first, then quickly he became more assured. When he left, he told me, "I'll take care of everything!" What's he planning? Why's he so slow in returning? These hours are like centuries to me. Ah! Someone's coming down the stairs! What if it were somebody other than Andrea?... No, it's him at last.

(*Andrea enters.*)

ROCAMBOLE: Finally you've returned! Do you have the safebox?
ANDREA: No.
ROCAMBOLE: No?
ANDREA: Here's your note back. (*aside*) He's useless to me now. (*aloud*) We won't need it. I've taken care of everything, as I said I would.
ROCAMBOLE: How? That's impossible! Baccarat now has us in her power.
ANDREA: Not at all. She'll soon be in ours.
ROCAMBOLE: But she knows the Marquis de Chamery is Albert's assassin.
ANDREA: And further, that he isn't the real Marquis de Chamery but a common thief called Joseph Fipart.
ROCAMBOLE: Who told her that?
ANDREA: I did.
ROCAMBOLE: Then, you've seen her?
ANDREA: She's here.
ROCAMBOLE: Here? In this Hotel? How did you lure her here?
ANDREA: I invited her here. Or rather, I had Albert invite her. She was so eager to see her former lover that

she came at once. Armand introduced me as Doctor Gordon, his friend, the man who saved his life, and in a moment, I had gained her absolute confidence. Your mother, whom I had brought and kept here, came to confirm all my declarations. She agreed to be silent over the past in order to aid your escape. But I don't want an uproar in my Hotel. A murder committed upstairs would leave traces; Baccarat must be lured down here.

ROCAMBOLE: What if she doesn't want to come down.

ANDREA: She will. I told Baccarat that that scoundrel, Joseph Fipart, had an accomplice, someone who has copies of all of the documents proving the birth and rights of Albert, the true Marquis de Chamery—and that this accomplice has agreed to sell them. In a wonderful display of generosity Baccarat, unknown to Albert, has agreed to buy them to insure the happiness of the man she loves—even though she, herself, is going to give him up and let him marry her rival. So, Baccarat is almost in our power, completely in our power. Wasn't that clever, my little Rocambole?

ROCAMBOLE: I admire you.

ANDREA: Thanks you! This old Hotel used to belong to a gang of counterfeiters—one the Police never caught. We're beneath the Seine. However loud one may scream, they'll never be heard down here. No one can enter here except through this passage that's sealed not by a door, but by means of an enormous stone that an ingenious mechanism either lifts or lowers. Once that stone is in place, no human effort can move it. Do you understand now why I want Baccarat to come down here?

ROCAMBOLE: Yes.

ANDREA: These counterfeiters were certainly clever folks!

ROCAMBOLE: You're leaving?

ANDREA: You have no need of me, I suppose.

ROCAMBOLE: Wait!

ANDREA: What do you want now?

ROCAMBOLE: I want–I want for you not to leave here without me–and I want to leave first.

ANDREA: Huh?

ROCAMBOLE: I don't believe in generosity. I know you too well. I know you plan to avenge yourself on me one day or the other–and perhaps this day has come.

ANDREA: Still suspicious?

ROCAMBOLE: You wish to get rid of Baccarat, so be it. You've prepared this tomb for her, I believe you–but it's big enough for two. So, I repeat, I don't want you to leave without me!

ANDREA: Come on, Rocambole! Sometimes, you display intelligence, but you lack logic. Would a creditor kill off his debtor? Don't you owe me my share of these five millions which you have hidden? Who but you can help me gain possession of this fortune? Are you reassured at last? Because I hear the rustle of a skirt coming down the stairs. It's Baccarat. Finish her quickly and come find me.

ROCAMBOLE: If you go now, you'll meet her.

ANDREA: No. The corridor is large and dark enough that she will pass me by without seeing me. (*climbing the steps*) Poor deluded fool who thinks me capable of ruining myself. One doesn't kill someone with five millions, Rocambole.

(*He disappears.*)

ROCAMBOLE: No, but one might kill the one to whom one owes five millions. There was a fine opportunity here and I missed it. Perhaps if I called him back–no, it's too late.

(*A woman appears on the stairway enveloped by a mantle and a veil; she slowly descends.*)

ROCAMBOLE: Baccarat!

(*Rocambole lets the woman descend without revealing himself to her; then, when she has entered the small cellar, he places himself between her and the stairway, blocking the passage.*)

ROCAMBOLE: Good evening, Baccarat. Ah! You weren't expecting to find me here so soon? You've come to buy the head of Joseph Fipart–of Joseph Fipart who now holds you in his power, and who won't let you escape a second time.

(*Maman Fipart–for it is she–reveals herself.*)

MAMAN FIPART: You were planning to murder her, weren't you? I did well, then, to take her place.
ROCAMBOLE (*awestruck*): Ah! Mama! You, here!
MAMAN FIPART: I'm not so easily fooled. I discovered your accomplice's secret–the trap set for Madame Charmet. So, covered with her mantle and her veil, I've come to spare you one more crime.

(*At this moment, the voice of Andrea can be heard under the vault.*)

ANDREA: Goodbye, Baccarat! Rocambole! I'm taking my revenge now—and it's well worth five millions to me!

(*Rocambole runs to the stairs.*)

ROCAMBOLE: Ah! The demon! The stone has been lowered. He's truly avenged. (*coming down*) The wretch! And I had figured him out—but now, I'm trapped in here.

MAMAN FIPART: Baccarat has nothing more to fear from you. And neither does Monsieur Albert. I know everything, Joseph.

ROCAMBOLE: Everything? But you didn't know that the trap set for Baccarat was also set for me, and that, like a fool, like a ninny, I let myself be caught—you didn't know that we're buried alive!

MAMAN FIPART: But Doctor Gordon said you'd be allowed to leave the country if you—

ROCAMBOLE: Leave the country? Are you mad? We're in a tomb, I tell you, and one doesn't emerge from a tomb. Here, look at this rock that no human force can raise, this stone that now separates us from the world of the living.

MAMAN FIPART: That's impossible. Doctor Gordon was your ally; he can't wish your death!

ROCAMBOLE: That man is more pitiless than an executioner!

MAMAN FIPART: Joseph, we must call for help. Our cries will be heard—someone will come.

ROCAMBOLE: No! No one will hear us—no one will come. That man has condemned us to a slow and horrible death.

MAMAN FIPART: Then, I thank God again for having inspired me with the thought of taking Baccarat's place. If you die, what need do I have to live?

ROCAMBOLE: Oh! To die–you–you who are not guilty? No, God cannot want that. Mother, my saintly mother, God cannot have condemned you to this horrifying agony. No–he will give me the strength–I will struggle–I will snatch you from this tomb. I am a wretch, a scoundrel–but I do love you, mama, I do love you. I will save you! I will tear my hands apart on these walls. I will pull out these stones, one by one. (*tries*) Oh! I can't, I can't. We're lost! We're really lost.

MAMAN FIPART: Let's pray to God, in that case, since he alone can come to our aid.

ROCAMBOLE: Yes, yes. I will pray with you, mama. You taught me to pray. (*falling on his knees*) My God! My God. Oh! I can no longer pray. I no longer know how to pray.

MAMAN FIPART: God, please send him your repentance and forbearance.

ROCAMBOLE (*suddenly standing up*): To die–when I'm young, when I'm rich? No, I shall not die! To die here and leave Andrea triumph, fortune and impunity? Not one witness left to accuse him–not one piece of evidence to condemn him? To die and not avenge myself? Never! God who strikes me cannot absolve him, the very man who made me into an assassin.

MAMAN FIPART: They'll come! They'll raise the stone.

ROCAMBOLE: But too late–too late! There'll be no one down here except two corpses. Well, at least this corpse can still denounce him. Yes–yes! But how to write? Ah! That card, that Jack of Hearts–he himself wrote his name on it. My dagger now. (*he pulls it from his pocket*) My blood. (*He pricks his hand and, one knee on the ground, with his blood, writes feverishly*) "Doctor Gordon is Sir Williams and Andrea de Felipone, the leader of the Jack of Hearts. He was my accomplice and he killed me. Joseph Fipart."

MAMAN FIPART: My God, let my death be the expiation for his sins.

ROCAMBOLE: Poor mama! She prays for me, she thinks only of me, and I am attempting nothing, nothing for her? Ah! I love her with my last breath. Inspire me, Lord, for her–for her. Ah! This metal rod from the press. I might dig a hole in this already crumbling wall. Yes, yes. (*embracing his mother*) Mama, mama, you won't die. I don't want you to die. We'll get out of here.

(*Rocambole climbs on the pile of stones that fell from the wall on the left and begins to attack the wall.*)

MAMAN FIPART: Lord! Have you then pity on us?

ROCAMBOLE: Oh! We will see again the light of Heaven. My God, for me I ask neither freedom nor vengeance–but for her, my God, life! Life! Ah, the stones are coming loose. That one's going to come down. Yes, yes! I feel a cold draft on my face. Air! Ah! My God! But what if there's water behind it!

(*A stone detaches, pushed by a stream of water which enters the cave through the reach. Joseph seeks refuge with his mother on the steps of the stairway.*)

MAMAN FIPART: Ah! Joseph, my child!

CURTAIN

ACT V

Scene VIII

The Hotel de Sallandrera. A pavilion giving on the garden. Andrea–in his Doctor Gordon persona–finishes a piano recital before the Duke de Sallandrera and Concepcion.

ANDREA: Now, Your Highness, you know why, only yesterday in your salon, I was saying to you: "postpone this marriage." It was only when these documents were in my hands that I could share them with you. It is proven that Joseph Fipart was an impostor–and that Albert is the true Marquis de Chamery.

CONCEPCION: My heart never deceived me!

ALBERT: Dearest Concepcion, this name, this title, are only precious to me because they bring me closer to you.

DUKE: I have no remaining doubts. Will we ever be able to repay you, Doctor?

ANDREA: Your Highness, by brother, Major Gordon, as he was returning to India, entrusted me with a mission which I've been lucky enough to accomplish. Joseph Fipart will no doubt be arrested sooner or later and will then be forced to return the fortune which he stole from the Chamerys. My task is now complete and I am leaving shortly.

ALBERT: Already?

ANDREA: Yes. Tomorrow, I plan to be in London, and from there, I'll return to India to be with my brother again. (*going to the Duke*) Goodbye, Your Highness! (*to Concepcion*) Mademoiselle de Sallandrera, may I?...

(*As Andrea bows, Concepcion offers him her hand which he takes to his lips. Suddenly, Tomas the valet enters and hands the Duke a card.*)

TOMAS: For Your Highness.
DUKE (*after having read the card*): Major Avatar? Who is he? (*to Tomas*) Show him in.

(*A moment later, Rocambole enters, now disguised as Major Avatar, dressed in grey, wearing blue-tinted glasses.*)

ROCAMBOLE: Your Highness, certain inquiries, which of which I have been charged by the highest authority, justify my presence in your Hotel. You have been deceived by an impostor.
DUKE: I know this, Major. Doctor Gordon has apprised us of the imposture of this Joseph Fipart.
ROCAMBOLE: Doctor Gordon, you say? My inquiry concerns Doctor Gordon...
ANDREA (*aside*): The Devil! (*to the Duke*) I must go, Your Highness. Please allow me to withdraw.
ROCAMBOLE: You cannot leave, Doctor.
ANDREA: I can't?
ROCAMBOLE: I have need of information that you alone can provide.
ANDREA: Me?
ROCAMBOLE: I'm conducting an investigation as a result of a complaint that has been made to our services.
ANDREA: A complaint? Who from? An old woman named Maman Fipart perhaps? (*to the Duke*) Your

Highness, she is the mother of the wretch who deceived you. A poor honest woman who did not wish, by being silent, to become her son's accomplice.

ROCAMBOLE: Our inquiries have established that Joseph Fipart was seen entering your Hotel, Doctor. What was the purpose of his visit?

ANDREA: Well, Major, if I concealed his visit, it's because I don't enjoy parading my virtue. That scoundrel Joseph Fipart knew that I possessed evidence that could ruin him. He wanted to buy it from me; he offered me a small fortune. But the Duke de Sallandrera and the new Marquis de Chamery know that I rejected his offer.

ROCAMBOLE: I see. Can you then explain, Doctor, how is it that Joseph Fipart entered your hotel but was never seen to leave?

ANDREA: He escaped, Major. The wily rogue ran away with the fortune he stole from the Marquis de Chamery. He left my Hotel, I affirm it. If it had been in my power to stop him, of course, I would have delivered him to justice. You have nothing further to ask, I suppose?

ROCAMBOLE: I have. I must now tell you that you are accused of the murder of Joseph Fipart.

(*General shock.*)

ALL: Doctor Gordon!

ANDREA: Me? The murder of that thief! Ridiculous! Because he has disappeared, because he avoided your surveillance, because he left my Hotel without being seen, you believe him to be dead and accuse me of his murder? And who is it who accuses me, Major? His mother, who in the fever of despair at having lost her son throws my name to the wolves? A poor mother whose sorrow has more likely driven her mad. Is she the one who accuses me?

(*Baccarat enters.*)

BACCARAT: No, wretch! I accuse you!
ANDREA (*recoiling*): Baccarat! Baccarat alive!
BACCARAT: Yes, Baccarat, whom you condemned to a horrible death! I was saved only through the devotion of a saintly woman who, knowing that a trap was set for me, offered to take my place in the cellar where Rocambole was waiting to kill me... Rocambole, Joseph Fipart, your accomplice, whom you wanted to eliminate, too–at any cost! Ah, I know you now, Doctor Gordon, or should I say–Sir Williams!
ALBERT: Sir Williams!
BACCARAT: Yes, Albert! Sir Williams, who used me to lure you to the Isle de Croissy–who dictated the very letter that led you there. (*to Andrea*) You no longer wear the same face, but you still have the same soul–that of an assassin!
ANDREA: Lies! All lies!
ROCAMBOLE: Water filling the cellar of which Madame Charmet speaks revealed its existence. When the Police were able to go down there, they found two bodies.
BACCARAT: Two corpses.

(*Jean Guignon enters.*)

JEAN GUIGNON: Apologies to all. One corpse only. I've come to tell you that our dear Maman Fipart is still alive. The doctor promised to save her. As for Joseph– well! For him, it was really over.

ANDREA (*aside*): Good! Rocambole alone could ruin me and Rocambole is dead. (*aloud*) Truly, this accusation is preposterous. What possible interest could I have in murdering this Rocambole?

JEAN GUIGNON: May I speak?

ROCAMBOLE: Please.

JEAN GUIGNON: You were Rocambole's master–the leader of the Club of the Jacks of Hearts. Also, you wanted the five millions Rocambole had stolen from the Marquis de Chamery for yourself. You gave me his note instructing me to bring the safebox I found under his bed to your Hotel.

ANDREA: I deny it all, do you hear me? I deny the murder and the theft of the five millions. Rocambole alone stole the money. Worried, not daring to return to his place, he must have arranged, without my knowledge, to have it taken to my Hotel. Later, thinking himself pursued by the police, he must have wanted to hide in the cellars–to flee with his mother last night. It's there that the flood surprised him. Yes, that must be what happened. That's what Rocambole himself would have said if he could speak. But the dead cannot speak.

BACCARAT (*producing a card*): The dead have spoken. On the corpse, we found a card upon which Rocambole himself had written–with his blood: "Doctor Gordon is Sir Williams and Andrea de Felipone, the leader of the Jack of Hearts. He was my accomplice and he killed me. Joseph Fipart."

(*Rocambole puts his hand on Andrea's shoulder as two more valets enter.*)

ROCAMBOLE: Andrea de Felipone, in the name of the Law, I arrest you. (*to Tomas and the other two valets*)

Deliver this man in the hands of the Police. (*to Albert*) The safebox retrieved in that scoundrel's Hotel will, of course, be returned to you, Marquis.

(*Albert turns toward Jean.*)

ALBERT: I have little need for that money now. I want you and Cerise to be married at the same time as Conception and I, and I want Maman Fipart to no longer have to worry about where her next job comes from.
JEAN GUIGNON: My luck has turned at last, it seems. All thanks to Rocambole in the end.

(*They leave while Major Avatar remains alone on stage.*)

ROCAMBOLE: All thanks to Rocambole. (*after a pause*) Redemption!

CURTAIN

The Adventures of Rocambole

by

Lucien Dabril

Characters

Joseph Fipart, a.k.a. Rocambole
Andrea de Felipone, a.k.a. Sir Williams
Louise Charmet, a.k.a. Baccarat

and in order of appearance:
Baron Kermor de Kermarouet
Colar, a.k.a. Rossignol
Comte Armand de Kergaz
Nicolo
Maman Fipart
Mourax
Monsieur Coquelet
Madame Coquelet
Edouard de Beaupréau
Cerise Charmet
Concierge
Thérèse de Beaupréau
Fernand Rocher
Hermine de Beaupréau
Jean Guignon
Jeanne de Balder
Léon Rolland
Bastien
Fanny
Police Inspector
PREFET of Police
Baronesse Angélique de Kermadec
Jonas
Chevalier de Lacy
Notary

The action takes place under King Louis-Philippe, in Paris, Bougival and in Brittany–around 1840.

ACT I

Scene I

A boudoir in the home of the Baron Kermor de Kermarouet: curtains and old tapestries, some 18th century furniture chosen with taste. Shoved into an armchair and enveloped with an ample dressing gown, is the Baron himself, a dry little old man, thin, with a yellow face whose eyes shine with a strange light.

BARON KERMOR (*calling his valet in a weak voice*): Colar! Colar!

(*Enter Colar.*)

COLAR (*very deferential*): Monsieur le Baron?
BARON KERMOR: My strength is abandoning me! An inner fire devours me. I'm suffering! But I must still live for one more hour. Have you sent the lad to fetch the Comte de Kergaz?
COLAR: Rocambole? Yes, sir–he's already been gone for three quarters of an hour.
BARON KERMOR: He's young. He might've become distracted along the way. And minutes are worth years to me!

(*Colar goes to the window and looks.*)

COLAR: Here he is! The Comte de Kergaz is with him.

143

BARON KERMOR (*hand on his heart*): Too late! Oh! I'm in a bad way. Run, quick! Fetch the doctor. Ah! Ah!

(*He falls over in prey to a violent and painful convulsion and remains stretched out.*)

COLAR (*very annoyed*): Damn Baron! All we need is for him to die without having made his will. I'll have to warn Sir Williams.

(*Rocambole shows up–he is a streetwise Parisian lad who has grown up too quickly; he allows the Comte de Kergaz to enter first.*)

ROCAMBOLE: If Monsieur le Comte will take the trouble to enter–
BARON KERMOR (*with a start*): Kergaz–I'm dying.
COMTE DE KERGAZ (*going to the sick man*): Baron– (*to Colar*) He's only got a breath of life left.
COLAR: I know a doctor who lives near by. If you will permit–it will take only a moment (*to Rocambole, dismissing him*) You can go now, Rocambole.
ROCAMBOLE (*boldly*): Not before having been paid what for my errand!
COMTE DE KERGAZ (*taken aback*): That's fair enough. This is for you. (*gives him a coin*) Now, go!
ROCAMBOLE (*looking at the coin*): A crown! Thanks, Monsieur le Comte! At this rate, I'm your servant. You have only to call for me, I'll be in the office.

(*Rocambole leaves.*)

COMTE DE KERGAZ (*looking at the Baron*): Poor old fellow–he seemed very troubled. What did he want from me? Kermor de Kermarouet. Neither the name nor the handwriting awaken the least memory in me.

(*The Comte de Kergaz takes a letter from his pocket; he sits in an armchair near the sick man and reads.*)

COMTE DE KERGAZ: "Dear Comte de Kergaz: You are a generous heart and you have dedicated your great fortune to doing good. A man tormented with remorse and whose last hour approaches begs a favor from you. The Priest whom I called to make my peace with God gave me your address and suggested you for this mission. Please come to me! My eternal salvation depends on it. Baron Kermor de Kermarouet, No. 3, Rue Saint-Louis." (*taking the hand of the dying man*) The pulse is irregular. If that doctor–
COLAR: He's here. (effacing himself) If the doctor will take the trouble of entering.

(*Sir Williams enters; he wears a white wig which contrasts with his relatively youthful face and holds himself bent over; he speaks with an affected British accent.*)

SIR WILLIAMS: Thanks. I'm Doctor Johnson.
COMTE DE KERGAZ: Comte Armand de Kergaz. You are no doubt, English?
SIR WILLIAMS: Irish. I don't practice in France. But I took care of this valet after a small street accident and he thought it proper to call me.
COMTE DE KERGAZ: I have no prejudice against English– (*gesture by Sir Williams*) or Irish doctors. But I fear that human assistance is already useless.

(*Sir Williams takes the pulse and examines the sick man.*)

SIR WILLIAMS: The case is serious indeed. The patient is in a coma. If I hadn't worked for a long time in a hospital, I wouldn't dare.... Excuse my boldness, but what I'm going to attempt today has never before been performed on a human being–only on dogs, as an experiment, but always successfully. Will you allow me?
COMTE DE KERGAZ: Please, do it, Doctor! It's necessary to revive this dying man–were it only for an hour. A good and great deed is at stake–and his eternal salvation before God himself.
SIR WILLIAMS: Monsieur le Comte, I am but a mere human–but I believe in Science more than God.

(*He raises the sheet that covered the Baron and takes an early type of hypodermic syringe from his bag; he then performs an injection on the patient.*)

SIR WILLIAMS: There! If my prognosis is correct, life will soon return little by little, his limbs will recover their agility and his brain its lucidity. But that revival will be short. A quarter of an hour, a half-hour, no more. Do use this time carefully, because after it, the patient will slip into his coma again, and will pass soon after.

(*While he puts his syringe back into his bag, the Baron awakens.*)

COMTE DE KERGAZ: Doctor! Look! It's a true resurrection!
SIR WILLIAMS: Excuse me. My work here is done.

(*He gets ready to withdraw, but the Comte holds him back.*)

COMTE DE KERGAZ: We may still have need of your services, Doctor. If you're not in too much of a hurry, could you be kind enough, in the name of mercy, to remain.

SIR WILLIAMS (*with a vague gesture*): As you please, Monsieur.

(*He sit himself discreetly at a table and leafs through an old book.*)

BARON KERMOR (*weak*): I'm–I'm thirsty.

(*Colar prepares some sugared water and hands it to him.*)

COLAR: How do you feel, Monsieur?

BARON KERMOR: Merci, Colar. I had a sort of vertigo. (*noticing the presence of the Comte de Kergaz*) Comte! I had totally forgotten your presence. We have no time to lose. A new crisis will be fatal to me. Come closer.

COMTE DE KERGAZ: At your service, Monsieur. You don't see any problem about the Doctor being present?

BARON KERMOR: None at all. I have a lot to say– and–

SIR WILLIAMS: Have no fear, I will be watching.

BARON KERMOR: In the eyes of the world, I am the last of my line: Baron Kermor de Kermarouet. I am leaving behind me neither parents, nor friends. The old valet who witnessed my birth and who, alone, would have been capable of weeping for me, passed away six

147

months ago. To my neighbor, I am only a virtuous old man, whose features they recognize, whose name they respect, but whom they will quickly forget. I said a virtuous old man, yet I'm hardly 53 (*lower*) and I don't deserve the respect which they give me. (*he seems crushed by his thoughts*)

COMTE DE KERGAZ (*encouraging him*): The approach of death doubtless causes you to exaggerate your sins. Who doesn't have some youthful peccadilloes to reproach himself with?

BARON KERMOR (*in a burst of energy*): I'm not talking about peccadilloes in the eyes of the world, but sins in the eyes of God. The priests' absolution is only good if I repair, to the fullest extent possible, the evil that I did. Thanks to you, I'm going to be able, at last, to unburden my conscience. (*he chokes for a moment*)

(*Sir Williams and Colar swiftly go to him and surround him with care.*)

SIR WILLIAMS: False alarm.

BARON KERMOR: I feel better, thanks. (*he catches his breath and continues*) I am rich, Monsieur le Comte. I have an immense fortune, almost incalculable. It alone can help me atone for my sin. In 1824, during the Spanish War, when I was still a sub-lieutenant in the Hussars, I was rejoining my regiment posted near Barcelona. I, and two other officers, traveled on horseback, in short stages, sleeping in towns, villages or in lonely inns by the highway. Here is what exactly happened to us on that trip. Two women, escorted by a Spanish muleteer, had just arrived–an aunt and her niece, the former already aged, the other a ravishing young girl of 20. Trusting us because of our uniforms, they went to their rooms while we accommodated ourselves of straw beds. We were young, Monsieur le Comte, we were drunk and we already considered ourselves the masters of this conquered land. The beauty of the young girl made a strong impression on us. Without knowing why, or how, one of us suggested an infamous deed that, normally, we would have rejected with indignation. Alas, the poor child was dragged to her fate. At daybreak, we were far away, leaving the girl dishonored. All I know of her is her first name–Thérèse–and this medallion, broken in the desperate struggle that she waged against us and which I thrust into my coat pocket. The next day, we came under fire and my two accomplices were killed. For me, life continued and the memory of my crime began to fade away. Later, I inherited my immense fortune from an old Jewish banker in Madrid who owed his to my grandfather. My ancestor had loaned 200,000 francs before he left for Spain. In return, he left me 12 million. I determined to scour the world to find Thérèse but I had barely moved into this old family Hotel that I became paralyzed. I haven't been able to leave this room for the last 20 years. Foreseeing the moment of my death, I suddenly thought–with the help of a priest–that the poor child I dishonored is, perhaps, still alive–and that there might have been a child– Do you understand now? Do you understand? (*he chokes anew, more violently than the last time.*)

SIR WILLIAMS: Hurry up. The action of the medication is wearing off.

BARON KERMOR (*to Kergaz*): Comte, you are good; I trust you. Take this key. Open the box placed on that table. You will find there two wills bearing different dates. The first creates you my residual heir. The second is in favor of Thérèse and her child...

(*Kergaz follows the directions of the dying man.*)

BARON KERMOR: Did you find them?
COMTE DE KERGAZ: Yes.
BARON KERMOR (*to Colar*): The crucifix now.

(*Colar brings it and Kermor places Kergaz's hand on the crucifix.*)

BARON KERMOR: Swear!
COMTE DE KERGAZ (*solemnly*): I swear on my honor to seek Thérèse and her child and to faithfully execute your last will.
BARON KERMOR: Thank you, Monsieur. I now die in peace. (*He expires.*)

(*Sir Williams closes the Baron's eyes.*)

SIR WILLIAMS: His heart has ceased to beat.
COMTE DE KERGAZ: I won't forget what you have done for this man, Doctor. Thanks to your science, you've been the hand of God.

(*Sir Williams makes a vague, acquiescent gesture; Kergaz then leaves.*)

SIR WILLIAMS (*to Colar, with no trace of an accent*): The hand of God–or that of the Devil.
COLAR: Compliments, Captain. You made an amazing doctor.
SIR WILLIAMS: I know my poisons, that's all.

COLAR: Now, the Comte de Kergaz, a man of wealth and resources, is going to seek the late Baron's heir. We must discover her before he does. Twelve millions! The game is worth it.

SIR WILLIAMS: The Comte de Kergaz and I are old acquaintances, Colar. He's a tough adversary. Have you sounded out some friends to help us?

COLAR: Yes, Captain. I will introduce them to you tomorrow at an inn in Bougival called the Rendezvous des Quatre Hussars.

(*They leave.*)

CURTAIN

Scene II

The Rendezvous des Quatre Hussars, an isolated inn on the banks of the Seine. It is run by Maman Fipart, an old woman with a husky voice, dressed in rags. She is usually enthroned behind a zinc counter decorated with a row of multicolored bottles. Square tables, wood benches and foot stools are strewn around. A trap door allows descent into the cellar.

NICOLO: A drink, woman!

MAMAN FIPART: Nothing doing. We're waiting for the Boss.

NICOLO: I don't give a damn about the Boss. I want something to drink.

MAMAN FIPART: Nicolo! You're drunk already. Aren't you ashamed?

NICOLO: I'm not. I'm still thirsty!

(*With some difficulty, he heads toward the trap door leading down to the cellar.*)

MAMAN FIPART (*to Mourax*): He's drunk–but not a bad man.

MOURAX: My word–that's true. When he isn't drunk, he's fine.

MAMAN FIPART: But when he's drunk, he fights! And he fights hard. Lucky for me, I've got an old carcass.

MOURAX: All the same, it mustn't be fun for every day?

MAMAN FIPART: Men are all the same. This one, that one–doesn't matter.

MOURAX: They're worse when they're thirsty.

VOICE OF NICOLO (*enraged*): Arr! You've locked the cellar again! Just wait, woman!
MOURAX: He's really mad now.

(*Nicolo returns and advances furiously towards Maman Fipart, ready to strike her.*)

NICOLO: Carrion! Dunghill! You know I'm croaking of thirst and you're refusing me a drink!
MOURAX: Christ! Here's company–fashionable company.

(*Enter the Coquelets; Madame seems to be an old flirt, Monsieur resembles a notary decked out in his Sunday best.*)

MONSIEUR COQUELET (*deferentially*): Enter Madame. It's here that Monsieur Colar said he would meet us. (*in a low voice*) I've got a hidden pistol in each pocket.
MADAME COQUELET (*surveying the other patrons*): I say, these men look rather repulsive.
NICOLO: See that dried-up hag that wouldn't know a man from a goat. (*to Maman Fipart, gallantly*) I like you even more, my beauty.
MAMAN FIPART (*flattered*): Heavens, that's a sweet thing to say. Here's a pint. Now, go sit in a corner and stay quiet. (*calling*) Rocambole! Hey, Rocambole!

(*Rocambole enters.*)

ROCAMBOLE: Here I am, mama.
MAMAN FIPART: Take care of these customers.

MOURAX: You're lucky to have that lad, woman! He more than makes up for the drunkard.

MAMAN FIPART: Oh, Rocambole has his faults too.

(*Rocambole goes to wait on the Coquelets.*)

ROCAMBOLE: What will the lady and gentleman have?

MONSIEUR COQUELET: Your best.

ROCAMBOLE: Presto! A bottle of Fifteen and two glasses.

MADAME COQUELET: What about my stomach? You're not thinking, Coquelet. After our meal, I want a Chartreuse or a strong Ratafia.

ROCAMBOLE: In that case, Madame, let me suggest a Crème d'Amour.

MADAME COQUELET: Smart boy.

ROCAMBOLE: Then, two crèmes?

MONSIEUR COQUELET: No. A Crème for Madame, but wine for me.

MOURAX (*to Maman Fipart*): He's very useful, though.

MAMAN FIPART: You bet. Shame he's not a few years older, he'd have replaced Nicolo. Colar says he'll make something of him.

MOURAX: Colar was in England with Sir Williams; he knows men. Where did that lad came from?

MAMAN FIPART: He came here one night to eat and drink. Then, he tried to leave without paying. I fell on him, but he soon had me under his knee. He took a knife from the table and I thought he was going to do me in. "Mother," he said to me, "you see I could easily dispose of you and carry off all your money and nobody would be the wiser. But I'd prefer to work with you. I've been alone too long–I must find a shelter. You can't be doing too well here; I'll give you a punch." He's a Devil, yes–but charming like a toff, so I took him in. (*pauses for a moment, then breaks off*) The old man's finished his pint. Take this bottle to him–but he'd better make it last. I won't give him another.

NICOLO (*seeing Mourax coming with the bottle*): Ah! Mourax, you're like a brother to me! Let's drink to when we were on the chain gang together. Mourax–to your health!

MOURAX: To yours, Nicolo!

MADAME COQUELET: On the chain gang! Coquelet–did you hear? They're former convicts.

MONSIEUR COQUELET: Fear nothing, my pretty; I have my pistols.

MADAME COQUELET. Oooh. I need a strong Ratafia!

(*Sir Williams, now looking like a large and handsome man of 30, enters with Colar.*)

MAMAN FIPART: Hello, Colar! Rocambole, take care of these gentlemen.

COLAR (*confidentially to Maman Fipart*): This is Sir Williams, my former Captain.

ROCAMBOLE (*pointing to a table far enough away from the others, near the trap door*): Here, you'll be able to see everything without being heard.

SIR WILLIAMS: Perfect.

COLAR (*who has rejoined them, to Rocambole*): Serve us some of your best champagne.

ROCAMBOLE: I've got what you want–1813, an excellent year.

(*He opens the trap door and goes down to the cellar.*)

COLAR: Well, Captain? What do you think of my little troupe?

NICOLO (*to Mourax*): How do you like the Milord?

MOURAX: What Milord?

NICOLO: The one with Colar.

MOURAX: He's got a determined look. I like that.

NICOLO: Me, as long as he pays well, it's all the same.

MADAME COQUELET: Coquelet! What a distinguished appearance that man has!

MAMAN FIPART (*aside*): If I were 30 years younger, I'd do stupid things for a man like that.

COLAR (*to Sir Williams*): I have picked the best. Over there are the Coquelets. It's in their apartment–Rue du Serpent–that the agency's office will be located. To the whole world, they'll be two bourgeois recently retired from business.

SIR WILLIAMS: Are they married?

COLAR: Nearly. Coquelet has a skillful pen; he can forge any handwriting, from the English style to the French round hand. They say that, when he worked as a notary's clerk, he imitated rather too gracefully the signatures of a few rich clients.

SIR WILLIAMS: An invaluable man, indeed.

COLAR: His wife poses as a model of piety and conjugal virtue. But if needed, she can play a lady of charity, a comtesse of the Faubourg or a Polish Princess.

SIR WILLIAMS (*noticing the incendiary glances that Madame Coquelet is throwing at him*): Let's encourage her to not waste her talents on me.

(*Rocambole emerges from the cellar with two bottles.*)

ROCAMBOLE: Presto! Here's the champagne, reserve stock.

COLAR (*ignoring Rocambole who uncorks the first bottle*): At the back are Nicolo and Mourax–joined at the hip, these two are. They shared the same bench at Toulon where they did ten years of hard labor. Mourax runs the numbers at the races on Sunday, dressed like Hercules, while Nicolo walks the crowd; they will serve us well. Mourax is gifted with uncommon strength and Nicolo is a skilled thief.

SIR WILLIAMS: Two collaborators of choice.

COLAR: Last, but not least, Maman Fipart, the innkeeper who, on occasion, can play the role of fence and trusty repository–if well compensated. Shall I present you now?

(*Rocambole is now hidden in the entrance to the cellar and listening to them.*)

SIR WILLIAMS: Have you found the villa I need?

COLAR: Yes. It's in Bougival, not 500 yards from here. A pretty little green nest, as much isolated as you could wish.

SIR WILLIAMS: Very good. We'll visit it after we're done here. Now, one last question, your terms?

COLAR: For everything?

SIR WILLIAMS: Yes. I hate trifling details.

COLAR: Ten thousand per month and ten percent of the profits.

SIR WILLIAMS: Agreed, but we'll have to act fast; my resources are not inexhaustible.

COLAR: It'll be a wise investment–with 12 millions fated to fall into our purses.

SIR WILLIAMS: I already have a lead. Since yesterday, I've spread the word among a virtual army of officials and clerks and now, I have cause to believe that the Thérèse we're looking for is now called Madame de Beaupréau.

COLAR: Madame de Beaupréau...

SIR WILLIAMS: Her husband is some kind of high civil servant at the Ministry of Foreign Affairs–and it's his daughter Hermine who's the true child of Baron Kermor. What remains is to get information about the girl and find the weaknesses of her false papa. If the Devil is with me, I will marry the innocent Hermine and the 12 millions are ours. (*rises abruptly*) Let's go inspect the villa. (*stumbles over Rocambole still hidden in the entrance to the cellar*) What are you doing there, loiterer?

ROCAMBOLE: I–I was awaiting the opportunity to offer you my services.

SIR WILLIAMS: You're an enterprising lad.

ROCAMBOLE: I can be most useful to His Lordship. (*meaningfully*) I know, for example, a very good Irish Doctor. (*a pause*) As for Mademoiselle de Beaupréau, I know that she's already fiancéed–to someone who won't willingly step aside. Finally, I have my ins at the Ministry, where many affairs are not all that foreign to me.

SIR WILLIAMS (*taking it in*): Hm. What's your name?

ROCAMBOLE: Rocambole.

SIR WILLIAMS: To me you seem like a wily little scoundrel. Well, you're hired. You'll report to Colar.

ROCAMBOLE: Hold on! I ask only ten percent of his share–one percent, if you will. I'm well worth it–or of his successor's share, in case of an accident. One has to plan for contingencies, just in case.

SIR WILLIAMS: What do you say, Colar?

COLAR: The lad has already rendered many services to me in the past, but I confess I hadn't thought of employing him in this matter.

ROCAMBOLE: That's exactly why I chose to introduce myself to the Milord.

COLAR: I think we can count on him. Agreed!

ROCAMBOLE (*slapping his hand*): Put 'er there! For life or death! And if you permit it, Monsieur? (*ready to renew the gesture with Sir Williams*)

SIR WILLIAMS: Why not? Yes, put it there! You please me, little rascal. I intend to make your fortune. (*throws a few coins on the table*) That's for the champagne, keep the rest.

ROCAMBOLE: Thank you, Boss!

(*Sir Williams leaves with Colar.*)

ROCAMBOLE: Now, friends, bring your glasses. The gentleman and the lady and you, too, mama. It's the Boss who's regaling us.

ALL (*toasting*): Long live the Boss!

CURTAIN

Scene III

In the street. This scene is played in front of a curtain or a canvas representing houses in the background while behind it a very important set change is taking place.

Rocambole is leaning on the wing at the left; Cerise, followed by Monsieur de Beaupréau, enters by the right, crosses the stage and disappears.

BEAUPRÉAU (*breathless, fat, ribbon of the Legion of Honor in his buttonhole*): Mademoiselle, Mademoiselle, I have two words to say to you.
CERISE: I regret, Monsieur, but I have no intention of listening to you. Goodbye, Monsieur!

(*She leaves.*)

BEAUPRÉAU: Mademoiselle! (*vexed*) Oh! She's gone into that building. (*in a paternalistic, condescending tone to Rocambole*) Young man...
ROCAMBOLE (*without a pause*): Yes, my fat friend?
BEAUPRÉAU: You must have noticed the pretty Mademoiselle who just went inside that house?
ROCAMBOLE: You mean, the one who refused to listen to you? Ah! Ah! (*imitating Cerise*) Goodbye, Monsieur! You didn't get it?
BEAUPRÉAU: "Goodbye, Monsieur!" It could mean anything. So what? Humph.
ROCAMBOLE: Yeah, right!

(*He leaves, beating a very dignified retreat. The concierge of the house, amused by the conversation, comes out.*)

ROCAMBOLE (*pointing at the departing Beaupréau*): Do you know this character?
CONCIERGE: No–why?
ROCAMBOLE: He's a fat civil servant who wanted to tell something to the pretty girl–the one who just went in.
CONCIERGE: Mademoiselle Cerise?
ROCAMBOLE: Yes, the one with cheeks like plump apples and a mouth like–
CONCIERGE: A cherry. Quite right. That's why she's called–
ROCAMBOLE: Cerise, for sure! What's the pretty girl do?
CONCIERGE: She's a florist, poor but honest. Her fiancé's a cabinet maker in the Faubourg Saint-Antoine.
ROCAMBOLE: I think I know him. Refresh my memory.
CONCIERGE: His name's Léon Rolland–
ROCAMBOLE: Right. Léon.
CONCIERGE: –and he works for Monsieur Gros.
ROCAMBOLE: It was on the tip of my tongue.
CONCIERGE: Mademoiselle Cerise is a honest, decent girl. Not like her sister.
ROCAMBOLE: Her sister?
CONCIERGE: A bad, bad girl. When I say she's bad, I mean it–a dissolute woman who wallows in fancy carriages and spends money as if it grew on trees.
ROCAMBOLE: What's her name–the sister?

161

CONCIERGE: She's called Baccarat, 'cause when she wears all her diamonds she looks like a Baccarat crystal chandelier.

ROCAMBOLE: Interesting. Do you know where she lives?

CONCIERGE: Rue Moncey.

ROCAMBOLE: Thanks! The day she invites me to lunch, I'll come and tell you all about her!

(*They all leave.*)

CURTAIN

Scene IV

A small, scanty room furnished with some pretentiousness, indicating social aspirations but no or little fortune. The characters are finishing their coffee.

THÉRÈSE: Monsieur de Beaupréau is making us wait. He seems to have forgotten our family dinner.

FERNAND (*excusing him*): One doesn't always do as one likes at the Ministry.

HERMINE: I'll be the last to complain because Papa is often grumbling.

FERNAND: If he was here, your father wouldn't fail to remind me that I came here to work on his great work about the law of nations.

THÉRÈSE: Which hopefully will help him gain the Legion of Honor and a considerable promotion. And all thanks to you, Monsieur Rocher, because left to his own devices, I'm sure he'd quite incapable of writing the first line of that boring old book.

FERNAND: I'm convinced that if he really wanted to–(*rising*)

THÉRÈSE: You are too indulgent! (*installs herself at a work of tapestry*)

HERMINE: Please stay a little longer, Monsieur Fernand. Will you accompany me on the piano. You'll allow me, Mother?

THÉRÈSE (*seeing that Fernand hesitates*): Well, since my husband is making us wait.

FERNAND: Thank you.

(*He goes near Hermine and sits at the piano.*)

HERMINE (*giving him the partition*): "Like the birds"– it's a pretty ballad. (*lower, very fast*) I've already spoken about our projects to Mama.

FERNAND: What did she say about it?

HERMINE: That we must talk to my father.

FERNAND: He will refuse me your hand.

HERMINE: Why should he?

FERNAND: Because I'm only Fernand Rocher, a low ranking employee at the ministry–not a match good enough for you.

HERMINE: Mama simply asked me if I was sure of your love. And right away, she promised me to ask my father.

THÉRÈSE: Well–that ballad?

HERMINE: Begin quickly, Monsieur. One, two– (*an elbow leaning on the piano she sings very simply*)

I

Hidden beneath the branches
Is a sweety of tweety
Listening to the murmur
Of the summer breeze.
The Sun through the branches
Plays games with light
Today is Sunday
Sing, little birds!

Refrain
Pretty lark, tender warbler
And you, Mister Nightingale
Who seems a bit crazy to me.
What are you singing?
Voices from the heart
Voices from the head

In "C" major or "si" flat
In key "fa" or key "sol"
What are you singing
There's no prettier theme
Than to say with you each day
I love you.
            Love
Yes, I love you and
I will love you always!

                    II
Sing the ritornelle
Of impudent liars
Your eternal loves
Won't last a moment
A passing butterfly
If it shines in your eyes
And you'll leave to hunt
For fabulous countries.

(*stopping suddenly*)
I'm afraid, Monsieur Fernand, that you'll be like the birds in the ballad.
FERNAND: My sweet Hermine, have no fear. I feel nothing but giddiness. (*sings, accompanying himself*)

                    III
They say he was swimming
By very big elephants
Loving life completely
Almost a hundred years old
Is he a better model
If you want to be happy
Faithful like them
And in love like them?

(*followed by the same Refrain.*)
HERMINE: Did you improvise that last couplet?
FERNAND (*very tenderly*): Yes, for you!

(*The abrupt arrival of Monsieur de Beaupréau interrupts this tender moment.*)

THÉRÈSE: You are late, my husband.
BEAUPRÉAU (*preoccupied*): Don't be alarmed. I'll be content with cold coffee–no sugar.

(*He lets himself fall wearily into an armchair. Thérèse serves him.*)

FERNAND: I–I am going to busy myself with the law of nations.

(*He leaves.*)

HERMINE (*low to Thérèse*): Me, too, I'm going to my room, mama.

(*She leaves by the opposite door to Fernand.*)

BEAUPRÉAU (*having swallowed his coffee in one gulp*): Heavens, where did Hermine and Fernand go?
THÉRÈSE: They left. Would you like me to call them back?
BEAUPRÉAU: No.
THÉRÈSE (*very sweetly*): Perhaps it's better this way. I have to speak to you about some serious matters, my husband. Hermine is 19, and if I can say this without offending you–you aren't thinking about it. It's the age when a young girl should get married.

BEAUPRÉAU: Get married, good God–what for?

THÉRÈSE: Why–because she won't always want to live with us–and–

BEAUPRÉAU: It takes two to get married.

THÉRÈSE: Yes. I think that–

BEAUPRÉAU: If you have a suitor in mind, that's another matter. Is he rich?

THÉRÈSE: Rich in good manners and other worthy qualities. And he loves Hermine enough to make her the happiest of women.

BEAUPRÉAU: You didn't answer my question. Is he rich? Really rich?

THÉRÈSE: Er, no–but he has an honorable career. You know him–you've been able to appreciate his services. It's Fernand Rocher–

BEAUPRÉAU: An employee without a penny to his name, without a protector and, therefore, a future. Are you mad, Madame? (*she begins to cry*) And there you go, crying over this child of fortune and immorality–

THÉRÈSE: Monsieur! Do not insult me! When you asked for my hand, you knew the truth about my condition. When you took that child in your arms, you said: "I will be her father."

BEAUPRÉAU: Haven't I kept my word?

THÉRÈSE: My daughter often asks why the man who calls himself her father only shows indifference–if not aversion–to her.

BEAUPRÉAU: It's natural that I would prefer my son– who is at school and for whom you seem to care little yourself. Be that as it may, know that I will stop this match by all means.

THÉRÈSE: Why? I'm sure that Fernand Rocher would make my daughter happy. And weren't you yourself poor as a churchmouse when I became your wife?

BEAUPRÉAU: If you insist that I consent to this marriage, there's something you must do first–

THÉRÈSE (*irritated*): You want me to disinherit her–

BEAUPRÉAU (*stubbornly*): I've recognized Hermine legally. Until she reaches her majority, she cannot marry without my consent. But that doesn't entitle her to–

(*Hermine rushes in and throws her arms around her mother's neck.*)

HERMINE: Mama! Mama! I heard everything. Don't cry. You're the best mother in the world and I'm proud of you. (*then quickly confronting Beaupréau*) Now for the two of us, Monsieur–My mother may be reluctant to disinherit me, but I have a right to renounce the money you're refusing to give me. The man I already consider my fiancé has a soul too lofty to lend itself to shabby calculations. (*calling*) Fernand! Fernand!

(*Fernand appears at the door; she takes him by the hand and leads him to Beaupréau.*)

HERMINE: (*to Fernand*): Do I have to ask you if you will accept me without a penny to my name? (*she doesn't wait for his response so sure is she of his answer*) Sit at that desk and sign a receipt for my dowry. It's on that condition and that condition alone that Monsieur de Beaupréau will grant you my hand in marriage.

FERNAND (*enthusiastically*): I'll sign!

CURTAIN

In the streets. Rocambole is with Colar who is dressed in a worker's garb.

ROCAMBOLE: So, Boss–is everything going the way Sir Williams planned?
COLAR: Yes, your information was good. I've been hired as a cabinet-maker under the name of Rossignol at the Gros factory, and there, I've become best friends with Léon Rolland, Cerise's fiancé.
ROCAMBOLE: Their love prospers?
COLAR: I guess so. They'll celebrate their engagement in Belleville next Sunday... Hey, look at that big lug over there.

(*Jean Guignon has stopped at the other side of the stage to light a cigarette.*)

COLAR: That's one of Léon's pals. Come this way.

(*As they disappear, Cerise enters; she carries a basket of artificial flowers on one arm and hats on the other.*)

JEAN GUIGNON (*delighted*): Mademoiselle Cerise! Where are you headed like that?
CERISE: To deliver my flowers. See how beautiful they are, Monsieur Guignon.
JEAN GUIGNON: Magnificent! (*advances, but suddenly utters a cry of pain*) Oh! There goes my bad luck again. I just pricked myself and my finger's bleeding. (*sucks his finger*)
CERISE: What a clumsy fellow you are!

JEAN GUIGNON: Not clumsy, only unlucky. It's not for nothing that they call me "Guignon." When I came into the world, I was no uglier than anyone else–but then I caught the smallpox. Later, I saved a few crowns to improve my likeness, but the tax collector got his hands on the money and it was gone.

CERISE: Poor, poor Monsieur Guignon. To console you for your misfortunes I'm going to invite you to our engagement party on Sunday.

JEAN GUIGNON: Léon is a lucky man. But can I tell you something? I wish he wouldn't invite the new man, Rossignol. He's got a face I don't care for. Just seeing him ruins my digestion.

(*They leave together laughing.*)

CURTAIN

Scene VI

A lady's boudoir decorated with lively curtains. The furniture new and a trifle gaudy. Cerise's basket of flowers is placed on a divan. Baccarat is trying on a hat Cerise has just brought her, before a mirror.

BACCARAT: What a delightful hat! My pretty Cerise, I'm proud to have a little sister like you.

CERISE: I'm less proud to have a big sister like you.

BACCARAT: Come on, I help my friends and they reward me for it. I love a bit of luxury.

CERISE: Don't you think it's more honest to behave virtuously and marry a brave lad?

BACCARAT: To live in misery–

CERISE: When you're with someone you love, you're never unhappy. Besides, Léon will soon be named foreman and he'll earn ten francs a day. As for me, I will continue to make flowers and, with our savings I'll purchase a dressmaker's shop.

BACCARAT: Why not ask me right now for the money you need to set yourself up in business? Plus, I'll order from you and you'll make all my hats.

CERISE: I don't want to owe anything to anyone.

BACCARAT: Be serious, I'm your sister.

CERISE: Yes, you're my sister, but you live at the expense of this Marquis and that Duke and who knows who else besides them. I'm sorry but I don't eat bread like that.

BACCARAT: For shame! You sow like a magician. This hat is so fine and elegant! If you knew how happy I am to be beautiful, my little Cerise.

CERISE: You don't need that hat to be beautiful–

171

BACCARAT: You can't imagine what's happened to me. I'm in love, my little sister, I'm in love, too! That surprises you, eh? I know all of Paris say that La Baccarat is but a coquette who hasn't got a heart. Well, I do have one. I'm in love, with a brave and honest lad. But because he is brave and honest, he pays no attention to me. You know him. I met him at your place. There are moments when I'd like to write to him or go up to his place and fall at his knees and shout: "Don't you know that I love you?"

CERISE: What's his name?

BACCARAT: Fernand Rocher.

CERISE: Don't you know he's engaged to Hermine de Beaupréau?

BACCARAT (*irritated*): Always obstacles on my path! But I will conquer them. I love him and he will love me, you hear me, or I'm no longer Baccarat! Your hat pleases me, I'll keep it. Here's 25 francs. Heavens! Don't thank me–it's the price I would pay Clotilde or Cecile.

CERISE: I already told you that I don't want– (*returns the note*)

BACCARAT: Keep the money, you've earned it. Honestly. Think of your shop. I'll be your best client.

CERISE: Charmer! (*hugs her. Bell rings*) A visit?

BACCARAT: An unexpected appointment. A new friend, perhaps. Would you like to meet him?

CERISE: Goodbye, little sister, I'll leave you to your bad company.

(*She leaves, taking her hamper of flowers. Baccarat removes her hat and quickly fixes her makeup. Then, Sir Williams enters, dressed very elegantly; he bows and takes the armchair that Baccarat offers him with a gesture.*)

SIR WILLIAMS: Madame, I am the Baronet Sir Williams.

BACCARAT: I entreat you–

SIR WILLIAMS: An indiscreet person has confided in me that you love one Monsieur Fernand Rocher.

BACCARAT: Let's forget about this indiscreet person, My Lord.

SIR WILLIAMS (*correcting her*): Do forgive me, but I'm only a baronet. In any event, if my information is inaccurate, I will be very happy for you.

BACCARAT: Because he is already engaged?

SIR WILLIAMS: Because it is always sad for a woman to see a man whom she loves escape her.

BACCARAT: Who told you he's going to escape me?

SIR WILLIAMS: So you do love him?

BACCARAT: With passion, with furor! He won't get married to anyone else, that I swear.

SIR WILLIAMS: Then, please accept my services.

BACCARAT: What for? To what end?

SIR WILLIAMS: Yes, I do have some interest in the matter... (*pause*) Perhaps you are acquainted with Monsieur de Beaupréau, who works at the Ministry of Foreign Affairs?

BACCARAT: I do not have that honor.

SIR WILLIAMS: Monsieur de Beaupréau has a daughter–Hermine–Fernand's fiancée. You would gain by making his acquaintance. Listen to him carefully and be surprised by nothing. He will tell you of his great admiration for your sister, Cerise. Perhaps, he will even let you understand that to marry her, he would even go so far as to divorce his present wife–

BACCARAT: I would throw him out.

SIR WILLIAMS: And you would be wrong, Madame, for he alone can stop the marriage between his daughter and the handsome young Fernand whom you desire. Don't protest! We are already allies.

BACCARAT: You work fast.

SIR WILLIAMS: I flatter myself on that. We must show the door as soon as possible to pale Hermine's would-be fiancé, and ruin him in her eyes with no chance of redemption. I make that my business. Take this pen and write: "My beloved Fernand, it's been four long days–long like four centuries–since your Baccarat has last seen you–"

BACCARAT: What's this?

SIR WILLIAMS: It'll all become clear in a minute. Just write: "You wretched man, you are not yet married and already, you are leaving me! I am greatly jealous of her, my lover. If you are not here, tonight, at my feet, I will go and make a scene before your fiancée. My lips on your lips, Baccarat."

BACCARAT: But–

SIR WILLIAMS: I think a small postscript is warranted. Add: "And don't dare make sweet eyes at my chamber maid who will deliver this letter." There. Now, the address: Fernand Rocher, No. 25, Rue du Marais.

BACCARAT: Here–it's done as you wanted it.

SIR WILLIAMS: Now, suppose that, by chance, this letter fell into the hands of Mademoiselle Hermine?

BACCARAT: I begin to think you are the Devil.

SIR WILLIAMS: If that were so, my beautiful friend, I would reserve a choice place for you in my inferno.

CURTAIN

The gates of Belleville. A small square lit only by the lights of a cheap winebar-restaurant pompously baptized The Harvest of Burgundy Harvest. First, we see a shadow: that of a workman passing by, whistling, both hands in his pockets–who disappears opposite. Then, two female shadows hesitatingly seek the restaurant.

JEANNE: The Harvest of Burgundy. Here we are.
CERISE: And we're the first. Let's go in!
JEANNE: No rush. The weather's nice tonight. Let's chat a bit outside while waiting for them.
CERISE: Aren't you afraid someone will hear us?
JEANNE: Kind Cerise! Would you hide your happiness?
CERISE: I am too happy. I tell myself that it's not natural and that a big–a very big–misfortune is going to happen to me.
JEANNE: Enjoy the happy hours of your betrothal in peace and without remorse, Cerise; your good heart deserves them.
CERISE: Don't you deserve some happiness too, Mademoiselle Jeanne? Your father, Captain de Balder, was killed in Turkey; your mother soon followed him to the grave, reducing you to earning a modest living by doing embroidery. I'm sure that God–
JEANNE (*stopping her*): He knows better than we what our needs are. Isn't that your fiancé?

(*Enter Colar, Mourax and Nicolo.*)

CERISE: No, it's one of his friends–Rossignol. And the two others, I don't know.

175

JEANNE: Let's go in. That Rossignol looks like a villainous character to me.

(*She pulls Cerise into the restaurant.*)

COLAR: You've seen her? That's Cerise with one of her friends, Jeanne de Balder. Léon won't be late now. Hide in the shadows, I'll point him out to you.
NICOLO AND MOURAX: Understood!

(*They hide in the darkness; the Comte de Kergaz emerges next, whistling and calmly crossing the stage. Then, Rocambole springs out of the shadows.*)

ROCAMBOLE (*to Colar*): You've spotted the man spying on you? Sure this isn't the Police or worse yet?
COLAR: What are you doing there, lad?
ROCAMBOLE: As you see, Boss, I'm practicing.
COLAR: Is it Sir Williams who–?
ROCAMBOLE: No, I've come on my personal account. (*very sure of himself*) If you bungle this affair, I have a plan for another operation in which we could share equally and which would contain none of the unpleasantries of this one.
COLAR: Go away. You'll bring us bad luck.
ROCAMBOLE: Don't bother about me; take delivery of your package first. (*to Nicolo and Mourax*) This way, friends–be ready–

(*He vanishes into the shadows; Léon appears, delighted to see Colar.*)

LÉON: Ah! Rossignol! What a nice surprise! This is my betrothal–celebrate with us.

COLAR: No can do, Léon. Some old pals have come all the way from my village. I can't leave them alone. Excuse me but thanks all the same! Good night!

(*He shakes Léon's hand and signals in passing to Mourax and Nicolo.*)

COLAR (*low*): That's him! Go! Go!
NICOLO AND MOURAX: Let's go!

(*Suddenly, the Comte de Kergaz reappears right behind them.*)

COMTE DE KERGAZ (*whistling between his teeth*): Bandits! You didn't count on me.
ROCAMBOLE (*who's seen him, aside*): Methinks the affair is compromised.

(*Rocambole slinks away as Colar leaves.*)

LÉON (*trying to recall Colar*): That's a shame! Mademoiselle de Balder's going to need an escort.

(*Nicolo goes to Léon and raises his cap.*)

NICOLO: Pardon, my prince, you wouldn't have a light?
LÉON: Yes, of course, I have my flint.

(*Mourax passes behind Léon and kicks him in the leg causing him to lose his balance.*)

MOURAX: The gentleman's not steady on his pins— He's already had too much to drink.

NICOLO (*pulling out his knife*): A little bloodletting will make him feel better.

COMTE DE KERGAZ (*pistol in hand*): Hands up or I shoot you both. One shot each for you villains.

NICOLO (*drawling*): What's up? One can't have a bit of fun any more.

(*Cerise and Jeanne emerge from the restaurant.*)

ROCAMBOLE (*seizes Mourax by the arm*): The trick's failed. Get out of here!

MOURAX (*to the others*): That's just what my friend was saying–just a little joke.

NICOLO: Yes, a joke. Come on, Mourax, let's go have a drink.

(*The two men beat a hasty retreat.*)

ROCAMBOLE (*introducing himself to the group*): Thanks to this nice gentleman, the villains have left.

CERISE: What's going on, Léon?

LÉON: I don't understand what happened. But I think this gentleman (*points at Kergaz*) just saved my life.

COMTE DE KERGAZ: I'd beware of that Rossignol, if I were you. I overheard him giving orders to the two wretches who attacked you.

JEANNE: I told you, Cerise. It's good to know who your real friends are.

ROCAMBOLE: In that case, Mademoiselle, you should thank the Comte de Kergaz who just saved the life of your fiancé.

LÉON: This workman–a Comte?

COMTE DE KERGAZ: Comte Armand de Kergaz, at your service. (*to Rocambole*) Who are you and where do you know me from, lad?

ROCAMBOLE: My name's Rocambole and I met you before at the Baron Kermor de Kermarouet's.

COMTE DE KERGAZ: My word, it's true.

CERISE: Messieurs, will you dine with us?

LÉON (*insistent*): Monsieur le Comte–

COMTE DE KERGAZ: On one condition, then–no more Comte. Only friends.

CERISE: Jeanne, offer your arm to Monsieur de Kergaz.

ROCAMBOLE (*aside*): Look at me now–I'm dining tonight with folks from on high.

CURTAIN

ACT II

Scene VIII

The Comte de Kergaz's Hotel. A simple room with yellow hangings. On the right side is a window. The Comte is seated on a chair writing at a desk. Bastien, his manservant, is before him. Only a corner of the stage is properly lit.

COMTE DE KERGAZ: Bastien, old friend, I've told you about Mademoiselle Jeanne de Balder with whom I dined the other night at The Harvest of Burgundy. Well, I'm now going to entrust you with a mission to her. A confidential mission, you understand, demanding all the tact of which you alone– (*rests his pen*)

BASTIEN: Monsieur le Comte knows how greatly I am devoted to him.

COMTE DE KERGAZ: Put on your best coat and go to No. 11, Rue Moncey, and see if there's a lodging to let. In the negative, slip ten crowns into the hand of the concierge to encourage one of his tenants to get out in 24 hours. Then, once this lodging has been found, take some furniture there and sign the lease in your name: Bastien, retired officer.

BASTIEN: Nothing very difficult thus far.

COMTE DE KERGAZ: As the house is inhabited by Mademoiselle de Balder, get information about her–but discreetly. If they answer you as I am confident that they will–that she's a young girl of good family, the victim of misfortune, find a way to talk to her. Your age permits it.

BASTIEN: Easy.

COMTE DE KERGAZ (*rising*): I gather her financial difficulties have forced her to sell her piano, so buy a second-hand one and add it to your furniture. Later, you will arrange for her to have it.

BASTIEN: How do I do that? The young lady might be too proud to accept–and if I have a piano, what am I doing with it? I don't play.

COMTE DE KERGAZ: Say that it belonged to your daughter–the daughter you lost–your only child. You have too much furniture, you can't find a place for it. You're forced to get rid of it. In fact, Mademoiselle de Balder will do you a favor by accepting it.

BASTIEN: Clever. Monsieur le Comte has thought of everything.

COMTE DE KERGAZ: Begun under such auspices, your relationship will soon become cordial and will enable you to learn many things. (*in confidence*) If I am not indifferent to her, as I hope, find a way to arrange a meeting between us. Act discreetly, for I tremble at the thought that Andrea, my half-brother, might learn of my new love. That evil man seduced the only woman I've ever loved and killed our mother. (*goes to the window and is startled.*) Oh! Bastien! Look at that man! What a strange resemblance! Was it sufficient merely to speak of Andrea to cause him to materialize?

BASTIEN (*looking*): Andrea had blonde hair and this man is dark–but he might be dyed.

COMTE DE KERGAZ: That demon is capable of anything.

BASTIEN: I'll go out at once and find out the truth.

CURTAIN

Scene IX

A private office furnished in an English fashion, rich and comfortable. Bastien impatiently awaits the arrival of Sir Williams.

SIR WILLIAMS (*entering*): What do you want with me, Monsieur? (*tossing his newspaper on the desk*)

BASTIEN: A moment of your time, no more. I was passing before your Hotel when you went in. I thought that I recognized you. But from what your concierge told me, you would be the baronet, Sir Williams?

SIR WILLIAMS: I am.

BASTIEN: Your hair's really dark for an Englishman.

SIR WILLIAMS: Actually, I'm not English, Monsieur, but Irish.

BASTIEN: Might have you been born in France? At a village called Kerloven, for instance?

SIR WILLIAMS: I never heard of the place. You are surely mistaken, Monsieur.

BASTIEN: Sir Williams, I believe that your father was Paolo de Felipone, who married in second marriage the widow of the Colonel Comte de Kergaz, who already had a son—your half-brother...

SIR WILLIAMS: I have no brother, Monsieur.

BASTIEN: This brother is the Comte Armand de Kergaz—as you used to be the Vicomte Andrea de Felipone.

SIR WILLIAMS: Stop this jest immediately, Monsieur, or I will ring for my men to throw you out.

BASTIEN (*firmly*): It's no jest, Monsieur Andrea. I know that I'm not mistaken. Your dead father, your brother have searched for you. Even though he was proclaimed sole heir to the Kergaz estate by decree of justice, he was ready to pardon your sins and share his wealth with you.

SIR WILLIAMS: Monsieur! I swear you are mistaken!

BASTIEN (*determined*): We're going to see right here and now if you're not Andrea de Felipone.

SIR WILLIAMS: I fear you've lost your mind.

BASTIEN: In that case, prove to me that I am crazy!

(*Bastien grips Sir Williams with his robust arms, then abruptly rips the collar from his shirt.*)

SIR WILLIAMS (*struggling to get loose*): Are you trying to kill me?

BASTIEN: No. I'm merely content with undressing you, for I know that you have a birthmark on your body–

SIR WILLIAMS: You think so?

BASTIEN: Under your left breast, a black indelible spot.

SIR WILLIAMS (*abruptly disengaging and opening his shirt*): No need for us to fight, then. Don't be afraid to look. Do you see a birthmark?

BASTIEN (*confused*): No... I...

SIR WILLIAMS: I continue to think, Monsieur, that you've been seized by an attack of madness–for your behavior towards me...

BASTIEN: The man you resemble so exactly is a wretch, capable of any crime.

SIR WILLIAMS: You see me flattered.

BASTIEN: Fierce hatred now separates the Comte de Kergaz and his half-brother, the Vicomte Andrea de Felipone. The law gave back to the Comte the rightful inheritance the Vicomte had stolen, but a man like Andrea doesn't renounce so easily. He will return at the first opportunity. I thought he had learned of the Comte's new love and that you were he–

SIR WILLIAMS (*interested*): Ah-ah. The Comte is in love.

BASTIEN: With the most noble, the most beautiful of women. But I've acted like an idiot. Monsieur, and I must apologize for–

SIR WILLIAMS: Just a minute, Monsieur! You've offended me. Don't be surprised if I ask your name and address.

BASTIEN: My name's Bastien.

SIR WILLIAMS: Bastien what?

BASTIEN: Just plain Bastien. I never knew my parents but I was decorated by the Emperor at Wagram where I wore the uniform of a Hussar of the Imperial Guard.

SIR WILLIAMS: Very well–Monsieur Bastien, from soldier to gentleman, there is little distance. I believe you will see no problems in giving me reparation by the arms.

BASTIEN: At your orders, Monsieur. A duel doesn't frighten a soldier. I live in Rue Sainte-Catherine at the Hotel de Kergaz.

SIR WILLIAMS: It will be impossible for me to send my second in less than 48 hours for I am not free tonight and tomorrow.

BASTIEN: Any day you please.

(*Bastien gives a military salute and withdraws. Sir Williams escorts him to the door.*)

SIR WILLIAMS (*now alone*): He thought me stupid enough to have kept that birthmark! Armand de Kergaz, you're ill-served and your attendant is a fool.

184

(*There is a knock on the door–it is Monsieur de Beaupréau.*)

SIR WILLIAMS: But isn't that Monsieur de Beaupréau? Come in quickly, my dear sir, I am anxious to hear your news.

BEAUPRÉAU: The news is good. By chance, Hermine has found–

SIR WILLIAMS: A chance in which you played a role–

BEAUPRÉAU: –The letter written by the mistress of her young man. She wept all the tears of her body and she's now prepared to write him a letter to break up their engagement–in fact, I dictated it to her. She left with her mother...

SIR WILLIAMS: Where to?

BEAUPRÉAU: Brittany. The ladies will stay for a time at the home of one of our relatives, the Baroness Kermadec. Young Fernand won't find her there.

SIR WILLIAMS: And for that to happen, he would have to be free, and I hope that–

BEAUPRÉAU: Oh, yes. I've faithfully followed your instructions again. I called him into my office to entrust him with the petty cash strongbox. I wasn't long gone when a messenger came to deliver Hermine's letter of rupture. The lad lost his head to the degree that he understandably forgot to lock the strongbox.

SIR WILLIAMS: And thus, it was easy for you to simulate a theft of which Fernand will be the supposed author. He'll be taken first to prison–then to the galleys.

BEAUPRÉAU: I've just reported the theft and filed a complaint with the Magistrate.

SIR WILLIAMS: Bravo! For the time being, Fernand's freedom is quite temporary; he's being watched by one of my friends. Tomorrow, the Police will investigate and arrest him. At the very least, until the Criminal Courts has decided his fate, he will no longer be of any concern to us. (*false commiseration*) Meanwhile, our first duty must be to console poor Hermine.

BEAUPRÉAU: When she learns of Fernand's crime, the cure will already be close at hand.

SIR WILLIAMS: Possibly. Yet, women are strange creatures whose reactions often surprise us. We must act very carefully. I have a sudden desire to see Brittany. Would you know of an opportunity to lodge in a castle near that where Madame and Mademoiselle de Beaupréau are staying?

BEAUPRÉAU: I am closely tied to an old gentleman whose mansion is not three leagues from the chateau where the ladies are going. And if you hunt–

SIR WILLIAMS: I do. You will introduce me to them and, in a month, as is proper, I will ask for Hermine's hand in marriage.

BEAUPRÉAU: Perhaps I should confide something to you...

SIR WILLIAMS: Dear, honorable Monsieur de Beaupréau! I know your affairs better than you do yourself. Hermine is the daughter of a man whose name you don't know. That man just died. He was 12 times a millionaire. I, alone, know his name and the location of his will–a will in which the name of his rightful heir has been left blank. If I marry your daughter, the will will be discovered, the blank space filled with Hermine's name– and her father-in-law will receive a nice slice of the wedding cake!

BEAUPRÉAU: I give you my word that you will marry her.

SIR WILLIAMS (*laughing*): Father-in-law, I think you're quite a rogue yourself. What a shame that your passion distracts you. Let me give you some advice–you must request a leave from the Ministry and rejoin your wife. Every day, you will send me a little bulletin on the condition of my future fiancée. By working for me, you will be working for yourself.

BEAUPRÉAU: That's indeed what decided me. As of tomorrow, I shall do as you say.

(*He leaves. Sir Williams goes to the window. We hear the voice of a newspaper salesman hawking his papers.*)

HAWKER: Evening News–five centimes. The latest news. Theft at the Ministry. Thirty thousand francs mysteriously vanish!

CURTAIN

Scene X

Baccarat's boudoir, same set as in Act I, Scene VI. The divan has been turned into a bed and Fernand is lying on it. His jacket and clothes are hanging on a chair. Baccarat, in a *negligé*, watches him.

FERNAND (*waking up*): Where am I?
BACCARAT: In the home of a friend. But you have a fever. The doctor has ordered rest for you, complete rest. You mustn't speak, you mustn't get up, you must be very good and reasonable.
FERNAND: What's wrong with me?
BACCARAT: You fainted in the street. I was passing by and, by chance, I recognized you.
FERNAND: How were you able to recognize me?
BACCARAT: And you–don't you recognize me?
FERNAND: Yes–it seems to me–you're beautiful. I must have seen you in a dream.
BACCARAT: Try to remember. I am Cerise's sister.
FERNAND: Yes, now I remember. It was at her place that I saw you.
BACCARAT: Now you're going to rest–sleep. And much later–when you're better–we will discuss all this.
FERNAND: Yes, much later. (*falls back on his pillow, very exhausted. And once again silence.*)
BACCARAT (*after a long contemplation of Fernand*): If you knew, if you knew how I love you, my darling! (*she leans over him and kisses him.*)

(*Her maid, Fanny, enters.*)

FANNY: Madame, a young man sent by your sister asks to speak to you.

BACCARAT: Fanny, how do you expect me to leave my Fernand? He could pass out any time if I leave him.

FANNY: Madame must be more reasonable. She's already spent the whole night standing up.

BACCARAT: I'm happy and regret nothing. If need be, I'll do more—and joyfully.

FANNY: But the young man—

BACCARAT: You're right. I can't abandon my Cerise either. Tell him to come in.

(*Fanny leaves and Rocambole enters almost immediately.*)

ROCAMBOLE: Honored lady, good day.

BACCARAT: Hush!

FERNAND (*half awake*): I'm thirsty.

ROCAMBOLE: Give him his sugar water. We can chat later. (*for a moment. he inspects the room*) It's nice here. (*then, as Baccarat has her back turned, he quickly slips a billfold inside one of the pockets of Fernand's jacket.*) The money is in place. The Boss will be happy.

BACCARAT (*facing him*): Now for the two of us, young man.

ROCAMBOLE: I had the good fortune to help your sister out of a difficult situation.

BACCARAT: What happened to her? Did Beaupréau—

ROCAMBOLE: He's still chasing her. The two of them have had a rather stormy conversation. You ought to see Mademoiselle Cerise defend herself—all tooth and nails out. I must tell you that I make it my business to follow all these little scandals. Anyway, no one's hurt. Your sister's safe and she wishes you good day. She told me to add that she'd be grateful to you if you could offer me a small reward, seeing that she's prevented by lack of money.

BACCARAT: I'm quite happy to know that she's in a safe place. (*gives him a few coins*) Here, that's for you.

ROCAMBOLE: Thank you, Madame. (*as he leaves*) Au revoir, Madame.

(*Suddenly, there is a loud knock.*)

INSPECTOR: In the name of the law–open!

BACCARAT (*scared*): The Police? Go open, Fanny.

(*A Police Inspector enters, accompanied by two policemen.*)

INSPECTOR: My apologies, Madame, for invading your home at such an hour–but I have come to fulfill a painful mission.

BACCARAT: Am I accused of something? I'm innocent.

INSPECTOR: Not you, Madame. But alas, someone you're sheltering under your roof– (*noticing Fernand*) Monsieur Fernand Rocher.

BACCARAT: Ah, indeed–who could have told you? What do you want with him?

INSPECTOR: The Police are always well informed. (*to Fernand*) You, get dressed and come with us.

FERNAND: Why–Monsieur–by virtue of what law–and why?

INSPECTOR: I'm executing a warrant issued against you this morning by the Prosecutor General.

FERNAND: A warrant–what have I done?

INSPECTOR (*harsh*): Get dressed.

BACCARAT: He's ill, Inspector. He'll catch cold.

INSPECTOR: A thousand regrets, Madame, but I'm only obeying orders.

FERNAND: But still–what crime have I committed?

INSPECTOR: Yesterday, the head of your department at the Ministry entrusted you with the petty cash strongbox. You took advantage of this to pilfer 30,000 francs out of it.

FERNAND: Me, Steal 30,000 francs? Never! That's false! That's false!

INSPECTOR: Your refusal to come with us would only aggravate your case by adding resisting the Police. Follow me with good grace, and if it's true that you're innocent, the investigating magistrate will set you free.

FERNAND: Of course he will. I still have the keys to the strongbox. (*takes them from his pocket and causes the billfold to fall from his jacket pocket, which reveals a bunch of banknotes.*)

INSPECTOR: And unless I'm mistaken, here are the 30,000 francs. Don't abuse justice any longer, my friend. (*pushing him toward the door*) Hola! Officers! Take this man away.

BACCARAT (*moved*): Fernand! I will save you, my love!

INSPECTOR (*gallantly*): Please excuse the inconvenience, Madame.

(*He and his men leave, with Fernand.*)

BACCARAT: Sir Williams did this! I'm sure of it, it must be Sir Williams! I'll tell them!

(*She intends to run after the Police but, suddenly, Sir Williams enters.*)

SIR WILLIAMS (*stopping her*): Bravo, Baccarat! But you needed to realize this sooner. The Police won't listen to you now that they've got physical evidence. I'm here to stop you from making a fool of yourself. As for young Fernand, he could be in prison for a long while–
BACCARAT: Monster! Bandit! Why did I ever listen to you?

(*Baccarat attacks Sir Williams, who easily deflects her blows and strikes her down. She falls to the ground. Sir Williams whistles and Rocambole returns.*)

ROCAMBOLE: I'm here, Boss.
SIR WILLIAMS: Excellent. You know your role.
ROCAMBOLE: Yes, Boss.
SIR WILLIAMS: Pretend to be her friend; do whatever it takes to remove her from my path. If she's difficult, have her committed at the Charenton Lunatic Asylum. Her name is Anais Heurtier and her madness consists in believing herself to be the notorious Baccarat.
ROCAMBOLE: Understood.
SIR WILLIAMS: Do you have the papers?
ROCAMBOLE: I do. The certificate of internment signed by two doctors from the Academy. A nice bit of work from the excellent Monsieur Coquelet.
SIR WILLIAMS: I'll be leaving now. Goodbye.

(*Remaining alone, Rocambole makes Baccarat breathe from a flask of salts. Little by little, she returns to consciousness.*)

ROCAMBOLE: Don't be afraid, it's only me, Madame. A friend. I'm here to save you just like I saved your sister.

BACCARAT: Rocambole! All this is the work of Sir Williams. A demon, a real demon!

ROCAMBOLE: No doubt, Madame. Your hotel is no longer safe; you shouldn't stay here.

BACCARAT: You're right, but where should I go?

ROCAMBOLE: How about, to find your sister Cerise?

BACCARAT (*dressing hastily*): Good idea! I'm coming!

CURTAIN

A square on a street. Mourax is dressed as a circus strongman and Nicolo as a clown with twirling batons; assisted by Colar and Rocambole, they are setting up a variety of props for their act: weights, dumbbells, drums, barrel organs, etc. Rocambole, a folio of songs under his arm, goes from one to the other, setting up the stage. Passers-by begin to pay attention, stop and form a half-circle.

ROCAMBOLE: Very fine! That looks good! Mourax, stretch your muscles. (*Mourax does*) Great! And you, Nicolo, batons in the air, ready for the parade. (*Nicolo assumes the pose*) Excellent! Now, Colar, to work! While you go about your business, the others will amuse the crowd. All the attention will be directed towards our group and you'll be able to work undisturbed.
COLAR: Rocambole, I can't call you my student anymore. Honest to God, I admire you. If you continue on this path, you'll go far!
ROCAMBOLE: Yes–to the galleys or the scaffold! Go on, hop to it!
COLAR: What I have need of you?
ROCAMBOLE: Two whistles and I'll be there. If all goes well, we'll be out of here in a wink.
COLAR: Understood!
ROCAMBOLE: Music first!

(*Drum roll by Nicolo as Colar leaves.*)

MOURAX (*very showman-like*): Come closer, ladies and gentlemen, come closer! We're going to show you the most magnificent spectacle of strength in the whole universe!

ROCAMBOLE: Come closer, ladies and gentlemen! For the first time in Paris, you will be able to behold the truly Herculean feats of strength of Eugene the Strongman, international champion and title holder of numerous medals, including two gold and three chocolate. (*drumroll*) Your attention, please! Go, Eugene!

(*Mourax raises successively three increasingly heavy halter bars with apparent ease, his overdramatic gestures underlining his strength and the weight of the halters.*)

ROCAMBOLE: Come on! Ladies! Gentlemen! Don't be afraid to encourage our champion! (*applause*) The crowd thank you, Eugene. And while you rest, we're all going to sing–together–"The Lament of Poor Mathurin." Music, maestro!

(*Nicolo abandons his drum for a street organ.*)

ROCAMBOLE: All in chorus to the refrain! (*He distributes song sheets and takes cash while singing.*)

Friends come hear the tale
Of a poor devil of a sailor
Who lived and died without glory
His first name was Mathurin
In swaddling clothes, without a note
Unworthily abandoned
They found him on a raft
In the neighborhood of Douamey

Refrain
Ah! The poor, poor kid
What misfortune he had down here.

ROCAMBOLE: Come on! Stronger–and all in chorus!
(*they all resume the refrain*)

Ah! The poor, poor kid
What misfortune he had down here.

ROCAMBOLE (clapping): Excellent! Excellent! Now,
it's Eugene's turn again! Watch closely, ladies and
gentlemen!

(*The Comte de Kergaz and Bastien enter in the
background. The manservant carries two swords under
his arm.*)

ROCAMBOLE (*to Nicolo*): There! The Comte de
Kergaz.
NICOLO: Doubtless the Boss isn't far off.
ROCAMBOLE (*pointing to Bastien*): If that fellow with
the swords hasn't killed him.

(*Meanwhile, Mourax continues his act.*)

MOURAX: Ladies and gentlemen–the next exercise is
particularly dangerous. These weights weigh
respectively 25, 50 and 100 kilos! Next, I will lift not
one but two weights of 100 kilos! (*drumroll*)

(*The Comte de Kergaz and Bastien cross the square,
oblivious to the show.*)

COMTE DE KERGAZ: My poor Bastien, Sir Williams clearly beat you.

BASTIEN: Yes. I behaved like an idiot and got beaten like a dog. He had me at his mercy. Why did he spare my life?

(*Three whistles cut through the air as Mourax executes his difficult lift with a certain dash. Rocambole and his two accomplices stop their act abruptly and look at each other. The crowd is first surprised then stupefied.*)

ROCAMBOLE: Colar's calling us. Come, Mourax.

(*Mourax and Nicolo quickly pack the drum, the canvas and the weights. Rocambole grabs the weights–with a light hand–to the great amusement of the crowd who then discover the weights are hollow! Uproar, laughter.*)

CROWD: Oh! The weights! All fake! What a comedy!

(*The Comte de Kergaz has noticed what's going on; he takes the swords from Bastien.*)

COMTE DE KERGAZ: Bastien, follow that lad, the one with the weights. His name's Rocambole. He'll lead us to the rest of the gang.

CURTAIN

Scene XII

The garden of a villa in Bougival. There is a round table and some rattan furniture.

MAMAN FIPART (*a bottle and glass in hand, toasting*): To your health, Nicolo, old drunkard! To your health, Mourax, you muscle-bound Apollo. To yours, too, Rocambole! (*each time, she swallows a gulp of brandy*) And last but not least–to your health, My Lord! (*she drinks from the bottle*)

SIR WILLIAMS: Enough mindless chattering, old woman. Go! Off you go!

MAMAN FIPART (*standing, with a scornful gesture*): Oh, you won't prevent me from licking the last drop.

(*She starts to leave, but curiosity distracts her as she suddenly sees Colar and Rocambole come in, carrying the sleeping Jeanne de Balder.*)

SIR WILLIAMS (*to Colar and Rocambole*): Easy–easy. Place her on that chaise-longue. (*he looks at her for a moment*) What do you say about it, Colar? A bird fit for a king? My worthy half-brother knows something about women!

MAMAN FIPART (*aside*): Another arrival. This isn't a villa–it's a harem!

SIR WILLIAMS (*who has heard her mumbling–with a gesture of riddance*): I said: be off!

MAMAN FIPART: This time, I think I understood!

(*She leaves, obsequiously.*)

COLAR: Should I wake her, Captain? Otherwise she'll be like this for a good quarter of an hour.

SIR WILLIAMS: Let her sleep! Take her to the pavilion. And place by her side the letter I gave you.

ROCAMBOLE: Right, Boss!

COLAR: Need some help, Rocambole?

(*They quickly take Jeanne to the nearby chamber.*)

SIR WILLIAMS (*reminding them*): Gently!

(*They return, without Jeanne.*)

COLAR: While we captured the girl, it seems as if you were fighting a duel, Captain?

SIR WILLIAMS: Yes—an amusement. I ought to have killed the man 20 times, but I preferred to let him escape with his life.

ROCAMBOLE: If you could have done it, you ought to have slain him, Boss. You always repent of having spared an adversary.

COLAR (*shocked*): This lad's a cynic!

SIR WILLIAMS (*pensive*): Perhaps he's right—if I'm mistaken, time will tell. Meanwhile, Colar, I need a spy in Brittany; I'm counting on you.

COLAR: I was dreaming of the seaside. This comes just at the right time. When do I leave?

SIR WILLIAMS: Wait—in several days.

COLAR: I'll start packing my bags.

(*He leaves.*)

SIR WILLIAMS: As for you, Rocambole, I have another mission. Maman Fipart is becoming impossible—I want you to be in charge here. I'll entrust you with our two pretty guests–Cerise and Mademoiselle de Balder.

ROCAMBOLE: As you wish, Boss. (*aside*) He trusts me.

SIR WILLIAMS: In fact, go and fetch Cerise. I need to speak to her.

(*Rocambole makes a hurried bow and leaves.*)

SIR WILLIAMS (*aside*): Trickster, cynic and liar–such is Rocambole. Why is he devoted to me? And for how much longer?

(*Rocambole returns with Cerise.*)

ROCAMBOLE: Come, Mademoiselle Cerise, I'm Rocambole, your friend, you know that. You've got nothing to fear from Sir Williams.

CERISE (*to Sir Williams with confidence*): It's impossible that all the harm they've done to me was by your orders, isn't it, Monsieur?

SIR WILLIAMS: Someone's done you harm? Who dared?

CERISE: I've been here for a week already without any news of those I love and–

SIR WILLIAMS: News of Léon Rolland, your fiancé? Alas! He's a brave lad who deserves your love. A day will come when you'll both be happy.

CERISE: I know quite well that this villainous woman was lying.

SIR WILLIAMS: I've kept you locked up here so that Monsieur de Beaupréau couldn't find you. And I ought to have made Léon leave Paris, for a great danger now threatens him.

CERISE: A great danger, indeed–bandits attacked him in Belleville.

SIR WILLIAMS: Was I wrong then to separate you from Léon? I'm entrusting you to Rocambole who will guarantee order and harmony here.

CERISE (*gratefully*): What have I done for you to be so kind towards me, Monsieur?

SIR WILLIAMS: The immense fortune that I've inherited serves me to do good and prevent evil. I, too, am in love! I love one of your friends.

CERISE: Jeanne de Balder?

SIR WILLIAMS: Imagine that there was a man bold enough to steal my name–a man who now falsely calls himself–

CERISE: –The Comte Armand de Kergaz!

SIR WILLIAMS: Well, this false Comte de Kergaz is none other than my former servant. The two bandits who quarreled with your fiancé had been hired by him to fool you. And now, he's succeeded in awakening tender feelings in Jeanne's heart.

CERISE: A former servant! How can that be?

SIR WILLIAMS: Once appraised of this trickster's actions, I discovered your friend's moving past. I fell in love with her at once, as one falls in love with the one of whom one dreams of giving one's name. But already, the trickster was forging ahead, so I had no choice but to have her carried off and brought here in her sleep.

CERISE: Jeanne is here?

SIR WILLIAMS: Yes. From now on, you'll be together.

CERISE (*on her knees*): Ah! Monsieur! You're as good as God himself!

SIR WILLIAMS: Arise, little Cerise, and listen to me. As soon as Jeanne wakes up, I'll be leaving–for a week. You'll be alone with her in this villa, where everything already belongs to she who will be the future Comtesse de Kergaz. I'll write to her every day. Allow my letters to have their effect–that and time.

(*Jeanne, now awake, enters and walks slowly towards them. Rocambole goes to warn Sir Williams.*)

ROCAMBOLE (*pointing to her*): Boss, Mademoiselle de Balder is awake.
SIR WILLIAMS: Hide for a moment so as not to surprise her. And take Cerise with you.

(*He leaves as Rocambole drags Cerise behind a hedge.*)

JEANNE (*alone, a letter in her hand*): This is all very mysterious. Am I dreaming? (*reads*) "I fought a duel but I'm safe and sound. I was near you just now, my beloved Jeanne, but you were asleep and I didn't want to wake you. I put a kiss on your face as a brother would kiss his sister, then withdrew silently. Trust me. You are at home, and soon you will be my wife–Armand" Armand? It can only be him. I love him.

CURTAIN

ACT III

Scene XIII

The office of the Préfet de Police in Paris. The furniture is sober, desk, tables, filing cabinets, book shelves. A curtain at the back imitates a wall posted with official notices.

PREFET: Please be seated, Monsieur de Kergaz. So, you saw this young girl, Mademoiselle de Balder, Tuesday evening. She appeared happy to meet you and rejoiced over plans for the future that you had sketched out together. Despite your reserve, she could have no doubts as to the nature of your feelings, and you thought, in good faith, that they were reciprocated. Is that quite it?

COMTE DE KERGAZ: Yes, Monsieur.

PREFET: In the afternoon of the next day, after the duel between Sir Williams and your manservant, Bastien, which you attended as a second, you wanted to see again the one you considered as your fiancée already, but you had the painful surprise of learning that the young girl had left her domicile?

COMTE DE KERGAZ: Yes. She'd been carried off against her will under the influence of a powerful narcotic.

PREFET: That's a supposition you're making.

COMTE DE KERGAZ: Not entirely. Mademoiselle de Balder's maid had been drugged, too.

PREFET (*taking a letter among his papers*): Still, the young girl left this note: "I am leaving to flee a man I

203

thought I loved, but no longer do, to be with another man whom I do love but who I cannot name."

COMTE DE KERGAZ: That letter is false.

PREFET: Perhaps. But you will have to furnish us with some evidence of that.

COMTE DE KERGAZ: I have it with me. Here's a short letter in the handwriting of Mademoiselle de Balder.

PREFET (*comparing the two letters*): Hm. If it's a forgery indeed, it's almost perfect. But if you're telling the truth, then this crime cannot be isolated. It may be but one in a series of other crimes perpetrated by a powerful and well-organized band.

COMTE DE KERGAZ: I understand your concern, Monsieur; still, I swear–

PREFET: You're relying on your feelings, Monsieur– but justice is only concerned about facts. Be confident, truth, in the end, always shines forth.

(*He rings–an usher enters, in whom we recognize Monsieur Coquelet in disguise.*)

PREFET: Bring Monsieur Rolland in.

(*Coquelet leaves.*)

PREFET: Another suspect recently mentioned a letter of dubious authenticity to us. And another gentleman came to see me this morning. He, too, mentioned Mademoiselle de Balder, a friend of hers, her disappearance and a theft at the Foreign Ministry in which one of his friends is implicated. Perhaps his case is connected to yours? You know of this affair?

COMTE DE KERGAZ: Only what I read in the newspapers.

(*Coquelet returns with Léon Rolland.*)

PREFET (*to Kergaz*): I ask you to allow me to conduct this interrogation in my own way. (*gesture of approval by Kergaz*) Monsieur Léon Rolland, right?
LÉON (*very moved*): Yes–yes–Monsieur–le Préfet...
PREFET: Don't get emotional, my friend.
LÉON: No, no, Monsieur.
PREFET: I've read your statement, and if I've understood you correctly, you're engaged to a florist?
LÉON: Yes–Cerise. Yes, Monsieur.
PREFET: You had to go out of town for business last week and, when you returned, she was gone.
LÉON: Well, yes–no–Monsieur–
COMTE DE KERGAZ: Please allow me, Monsieur le Préfet. I know this brave lad, and through the greatest of luck, I was present at his engagement dinner with Mademoiselle Cerise.
LÉON: That's–that's true. I–Monsieur le Comte de Kergaz.
COMTE DE KERGAZ: It was precisely at this very dinner that I made the acquaintance of Mademoiselle de Balder. I had, in fact, intervened earlier to thwart an attack against this brave lad here.
PREFET: These events are too coincidental not to be connected.
LÉON: I–I thought that perhaps–Baccarat might know–
PREFET: La Baccarat? That woman of flashy dresses and loose morals at whose home Fernand Rocher was arrested?
LÉON: Yes, Monsieur. You see–she's–she's Cerise's sister. I thought that if something bad had happened to Cerise, she'd know. So, I went to her place and I rang

the bell, but a joker shouted at me from the corner of the street: "You're wasting your fist, no one's at home."

PREFET (*uneasily*): So she, too, has disappeared–

COMTE DE KERGAZ: You think that–

PREFET: At the very least, her disappearance might be an admission of guilt. Because of the–support–she enjoys amongst the high society, I didn't want to implicate her in the affair of the theft. All this is very worrisome.

(*Coquelet returns discreetly and delivers a request for an audience to the PREFET.*)

COQUELET: I'm told this is very urgent.

PREFET (*after having read*): Speak of the Devil! It's she–Baccarat! (*to Coquelet*) Show her in!

(*Coquelet lets Baccarat in, then leaves.*)

PREFET (*to Baccarat*): You can speak before these gentlemen as if I were alone.

BACCARAT: I thank you, Monsieur le Préfet, for seeing me so promptly. Look at my face, as you look at the faces of criminals, and tell me if I look like a thief?

PREFET: No, assuredly not.

BACCARAT: Well, be assured that Fernand Rocher, the young man whom your men arrested in my apartment, is as innocent as I am of the theft of which he's accused.

PREFET: These are heavy charges against him.

BACCARAT: I know.

PREFET: Overwhelming material evidence–

BACCARAT (*very much at ease*): False or faked so as to be worthless! Oh! My own role is still not very proper in this affair. I clumsily played an unwitting part in the chain of events that led him to being accused. I wrote the letter which made it look as if Fernand was being unfaithful to his fiancée. And I also wrote the letter which was used to lure my sister into a trap. But I swear that I only undertook these villainies under the guidance of a man known as the Baronet Sir Williams. He, alone, is guilty.

COMTE DE KERGAZ: What a curious coincidence! It was against Sir Williams that my servant Bastien fought a duel, and it was during this duel that Mademoiselle de Balder was carried off.

BACCARAT: That man is a demon. He used me like a toy, then he had me locked-up in a mad house. But I managed to escape–and I will atone for my sins by rescuing Fernand from prison.

PREFET (*to her, as he writes*): You seem sincere, Madame. This warrants further investigation...

(*He rings for the usher and gives him a note.*)

PREFET: Quick, go down to the lock up. Bring Fernand Rocher here without delay.

COQUELET: Yes, Monsieur le Préfet.

(*He leaves.*)

LÉON (*who has gone to Baccarat*): Madame, do you have news of Cerise?

BACCARAT: None, alas! I am a wretch.

LÉON: My–my fiancée– (*bursts into tears*)

(*Coquelet returns with a handcuffed Fernand, surrounded by two policemen.*)

207

COQUELET: Here's the prisoner, Monsieur le Préfet.

PREFET (*to the policemen*): Uncuff him–but keep a close eye on him.

FERNAND: What do you want with me? Why are you bothering me? Let me be freed of this life which weighs on me. (*noticing Baccarat*) Ah–I understand–a whim of Madame. She dares to pursue me even here!

BACCARAT: Monsieur, you have every right to scorn me. Still, I am the means of proving your innocence.

FERNAND: You, who ruined me?

BACCARAT: I have been unworthy of your trust, I admit it. One day, my sister told me that you were going to marry Mademoiselle Hermine de Beaupréau. I spent a sleepless night, moved by a thousand confused thoughts; then, I lost my head and all control of my actions. That morning, Sir Williams introduced himself to me and said to me, "You love Fernand, I love Mademoiselle de Beaupréau." And later, Monsieur de Beaupréau added, "I love Cerise and I'm ready to divorce my wife to marry her. Help me." After that, I became an instrument in their evil hands.

FERNAND: I think I'm beginning to understand.

BACCARAT: Sir Williams dictated a letter to me in which I treated you as if you were my lover. Then, Monsieur de Beaupréau let it be discovered by Mademoiselle Hermine at home. Ruined in her eyes, it was still necessary to ruin you in the eyes of the world. With Monsieur de Beaupréau's help again, Sir Williams was able to stimulate the theft of 30,000 francs. Yes, he alone planned everything. And I can prove it.

PREFET (*severely*): Madame, as surely you must realize, your allegations are exceedingly serious. If you're telling the truth, a top-ranking official of the Foreign Affairs Ministry will find himself gravely compromised. And that Sir Williams you accuse so forcefully is a subject of the British Crown, whom I'm sure the English Ambassador will defend and protect.

COMTE DE KERGAZ: Allow me to ask you a question, Monsieur Rocher. Was Mademoiselle Hermine your fiancée rich?

FERNAND: Not at all. In fact, Monsieur de Beaupréau only consented to grant me her hand on the condition that she married me without a dowry. Indeed, Monsieur de Beaupréau is not Hermine's true father...

COMTE DE KERGAZ: Madame de Beaupréau had remarried?

FERNAND: I don't know. I don't think so. I think rather that she had–committed a fault–

COMTE DE KERGAZ: My God! If it were she! Do you know the first name of Madame de Beaupréau?

FERNAND: Yes, her name's Thérèse.

COMTE DE KERGAZ: Thérèse! Monsieur le Préfet, I think I've got the key to the entire mystery. Mademoiselle Hermine de Beaupréau is the natural daughter of Baron Kermor de Kermarouet. All the events, all the crimes that have puzzled us have no other purpose than the embezzlement of the late Baron's inheritance–12 millions francs!

PREFET: Twelve millions! But this Sir Williams?

COMTE DE KERGAZ: A false British subject that I will assist you in unmasking.

PREFET: So you know who he is?

COMTE DE KERGAZ: To my shame, yes. He's my half-brother, the Vicomte Andrea de Felipone. His father murdered mine to steal his wife from him.

CURTAIN

Scene XIV

The Rendezvous des Quatre Hussars. Same décor as in Act I, Scene II. Full night. The hovel is lit only by a few smoking candles.

MAMAN FIPART (*sitting behind the counter as Rocambole who enters*): Where's Colar?

ROCAMBOLE: He'll be here soon with Léon (*to Nicolo and Mourax*) Don't bungle the job, this time.

NICOLO (*to Maman Fipart*): Give us a drink so we'll have some courage for the job.

ROCAMBOLE (*putting on a blue apron*): Hold on! No bottle yet! If you succeed, then you'll get as much wine as you like.

MOURAX: Then let's hurry!

ROCAMBOLE: Hush! Here he is!

(*Colar enters with Léon Rolland.*)

COLAR: Hello, Maman! I've come with a friend of mine to have a drink.

MAMAN FIPART: Fine. You know the customs of the house.

LÉON (*to Colar*): You are a habitué?

COLAR: I was–yes. The wine here is good and the food copious. Let's a bit.

(*They both sit at a table.*)

LÉON: You know, I've come here only because of Cerise.

MAMAN FIPART: Rocambole, serve Colar and his guest.

LÉON: Say there, Rossignol, she's calling you Colar.

(*Vague gesture by Colar who doesn't appear to be concerned about it.*)

ROCAMBOLE: What will the gentlemen have?

COLAR: A bottle of red and some cheese.

LÉON: Rocambole–Rocambole–I know him. He dined with us that famous evening in Belleville.

COLAR: There, you see, you're in good company here.

ROCAMBOLE (*returning with the food*): Presto!

LÉON: Hey, lad! You remember Belleville?

ROCAMBOLE (*falsely surprised*): Monsieur Léon! What a surprise! Yes, indeed.

COLAR: Rocambole, would you like to earn some money? (pulls out two 100-*sou* coins)

ROCAMBOLE: That's nothing to frown at.

COLAR: What's the news hereabouts?

ROCAMBOLE: The installation of an English millionaire–Sir Williams, as he's called.

LÉON (*aside*): Sir Williams. That's indeed the name Baccarat spoke of.

COLAR: Where does he live, this Englishman?

ROCAMBOLE: In a villa on the heights of Bougival.

COLAR: Is he married or single?

ROCAMBOLE: I've heard it said that there are women in the villa. There's one they call–Marquise or something like that.

LÉON: Cerise–it's she.

ROCAMBOLE: Cerise–that's it, I should have remembered it.

MAMAN FIPART: Rocambole!

ROCAMBOLE: Coming, Mama!

MAMAN FIPART (*pointing to Nicolo and Mourax*): Those gentlemen must be served, too.

ROCAMBOLE (*going to the table*): Open your eyes and watch carefully.

COLAR (*to Léon*): This is a convenient place. People could be murdered here and no one would know anything about it. The river is two steps away and the wheels of the watermills at Marly turn ceaselessly. They could throw a man into the water there and the wheels would chop him to ribbons and after that, no one could tell if it was a crime or an accident.

LÉON: Why are you telling me this?

NICOLO (*to Mourax*): To strangle a customer, you've got to grab him properly by the neck with your hands and then, you press your thumbs hard–very hard–

LÉON (*who has heard, uneasily*): They're speaking of murder.

COLAR: Getting rid of folks who bother you isn't always a crime. Suppose you bothered me, you being friend with folks who're being a pain–like the Comte de Kergaz...

LÉON: You know him?

COLAR: It's just a supposition. Well, I'd bring you here one night just like tonight; some friends of mine would already be here, and when I'd judge the moment to be opportune, I'd stand up and shout, "Hey, I've got our pigeon!"

(*Colar suddenly grabs Léon who struggles. Nicolo and Mourax come to help him.*)

LÉON: Wretch! Do you intend to murder me?

COLAR: Sure! You bother me!

LÉON: Scum!

(*Léon succeeds in freeing himself with a kidney punch; he grabs a knife, gets his back to a window and pulls a table in front of him.*)

LÉON: Help me, Rocambole!
MAMAN FIPART: This is going all wrong!
ROCAMBOLE (*to Maman Fipart*): Don't be afraid, Mama! Pretend to be old and feeble and hang on my coat. (*waves to emphasize his helplessness and shouts*) Courage, Léon!
LÉON: I'll need it! But I'll sell my skin dearly.
COLAR: Listen, pal, don't make so much noise. Since your fate is settled, you might as well accept it gracefully.
LÉON: Not before I kill at least one of you. (*with a blow of his elbow, he breaks one of the panes of the window*) Help! Help!
ROCAMBOLE: Thief! Murder!
COLAR: Shut up! You two, hurry! Let's get it over with!
NICOLO (*hurling a bottle which shatters on Léon's head*): Here! Take this!
MOURAX: Well aimed!

(*Suddenly, a shot is fired from outside; the window opens as Colar collapses. The Comte de Kergaz jumps through the window, as Nicolo and Mourax slip under the tables.*)

COMTE DE KERGAZ: Hands up!

213

ROCAMBOLE: I can't–the old woman's holding on to me for her dear life. Besides, we're old acquaintances, Monsieur le Comte.

NICOLO (*low to Mourax*): Come on! Let's beat it!

(*Nicolo leaps through the window, but Mourax stumbles. The Comte de Kergaz fires a shot in his direction. Mourax plays dead, then taking advantage of Kergaz's distraction, he manages to flee.*)

COMTE DE KERGAZ (*leaning over Colar*): Rocambole, bring me a napkin and some water!

ROCAMBOLE: Right, Boss!

COMTE DE KERGAZ (*to Colar after wiping his face*): Do you have something to say before dying?

COLAR: I paid my dues. Others will avenge me.

KERGAZ: Wretch! Where have I seen your ugly face before? Ah, yes! You were one of the servants at Baron Kermor's home! You and your master, you knew the secret. (*seeing that he's speaking in vain, he leaves him and rises*) He's dead. Rocambole knows, perhaps. (*to Rocambole*) Would you like to earn some money, lad?

ROCAMBOLE: That's nothing to frown at.

COMTE DE KERGAZ: Do you know where to find Cerise and Mademoiselle de Balder?

ROCAMBOLE: They're barely ten minutes from here. That piece of information's worth 50 crowns.

COMTE DE KERGAZ: Well, here's ten on account. The rest will be given to you when I've located the two ladies.

ROCAMBOLE: Well, they're on an island. Follow me to the gangway of the watermills. I'll point out the way.

COMTE DE KERGAZ (*to Léon who seems to emerge from a long sleep*): Come, Léon, the fresh air will do you good.

(*Kergaz helps Léon to get up.*)

ROCAMBOLE (*to Maman Fipart*): Have no fear, Mama! I'm going to play them a trick of my own.

CURTAIN

Scene XV

A crossroad somewhere in the Breton countryside

SIR WILLIAMS (*to Monsieur de Beaupréau who arrives from the opposite direction*): Congratulations, you're right on time.

BEAUPRÉAU: Being on time is the chief quality of a good civil servant.

SIR WILLIAMS: I will get you a promotion. (*shakes his hand*) Can I risk myself at your aunt's?

BEAUPRÉAU: The moment is most favorable. Hermine's forgotten Fernand or, at least, no longer speaks of him. My wife is well acquainted with you. And the old aunt dreams of entertaining fancy guests. They're ready for you.

SIR WILLIAMS: When will you introduce me?

BEAUPRÉAU: This evening at the Saut-du-Moine, halfway between Saint Malo and Castle des Genets. Be there.

SIR WILLIAMS: Why there?

BEAUPRÉAU: Because that place is the wildest and the most romantic along the cliffs. If these ladies first meet you there, with a sad and forlorn air, they'll become besotted with you.

SIR WILLIAMS: I have an even better idea, father-in-law. I'll pretend to save your life–say, from your runaway horse which might otherwise throw itself over the cliff.

BEAUPRÉAU: My son-in-law, you have excellent ideas–but doesn't that sound a trifle risky?

SIR WILLIAMS: Don't worry–I wish you only good.

BEAUPRÉAU: In that case, let's speak of Cerise.

SIR WILLIAMS: Your clumsiness has almost ruined everything–but she is actually under good care–together, we will succeed in this enterprise...

(*They leave arm in arm.*)

CURTAIN

Scene XVI

A small room in the Chateau des Genets A few curtains of old silk, a window, some furniture– including a piano. Baronesse Angélique de Kermadec, a sprightly 84, listens to a novel of chivalry which Jonas, a bald old servant with a white beard, recites to her.

KERMADEC: Continue, Jonas. Your voice is a little trembling, but you've never read me anything so engaging. Continue.

JONAS (*reading*): "The queen was the most beautiful woman that ever was. Near her, a young page began to sing to the accompaniment of a harp so melodious that the queen sat down to listen to him. As he finished, the queen leaned out the window and saw a beautiful man in the outfit of a knight errant. Leaping from his black horse, the knight set foot on the ground and, spying the queen at her window, bent his knee and bowed to her so deeply that his face was almost touching the ground. And while she smiled and looked at the knight, the queen's hand wandered for a moment in the hand of the page, whose heart began to beat violently..."

KERMADEC (*she has placed her hand instinctively on Jonas's head*): Ah! Listening to you, it's as if I a lady of honor to Queen Marie-Antoinette again, and the knight errant... (*she goes to the window and exclaims abruptly enlightened*) He's here! He's just noticed me and is bowing to me!

JONAS: He's supposed to bend his knee and his face almost touch the ground.

KERMADEC: Go and let this gentleman in!

(*Jonas leaves, stupefied, as the Baroness claps her hands.*)

KERMADEC: Oh! How delighted I am! How delighted I am! It's been 20 years since I've seen such a handsome man. It was—it was in a small inn in a little Spanish village. I was coming back from taking the waters at Salies, and my niece, Thérèse, was accompanying me. And that night, a Hussar lieutenant—

(*Jonas returns.*)

JONAS: Madame, the "knight" was lost in the woods. As night is falling, he solicits your hospitality until the morrow.
KERMADEC: Is it necessary to tell you again, Jonas, that my chateau is open to him. Introduce him and light the torches.

(*Jonas leaves and soon introduces Sir Williams.*)

SIR WILLIAMS (*saluting the Baronesse with style*): Pardon, Dear Madame, my indiscretion—
KERMADEC: Monsieur, for many centuries, errant knights and weary pilgrims have found asylum in this castle. Do like them.

(*Jonas lights candles in the salon and then retires.*)

SIR WILLIAMS: I was going to the manor of Monsieur de Lacy—and I am unaware of—
KERMADEC: You know the Chevalier de Lacy?
SIR WILLIAMS: His nephew is one of my best friends.

KERMADEC: I hope, in that case, that we will see each other often.

SIR WILLIAMS: Allow me to introduce myself: I am the Baronet Sir Williams, of Irish ancestry.

KERMADEC: And I, the Baronesse Angélique de Kermadec, of pure Breton stock.

SIR WILLIAMS: Your warm hospitality is particularly appreciated at this time, for I'm plagued by dark thoughts which haunt me like the memory of some unforgivable sin.

KERMADEC: May I–dare I ask what tortures you so?.

SIR WILLIAMS: Alas! I love a woman who is unable to return my love.

KERMADEC: Poor man.

SIR WILLIAMS: I thought myself far away from her, and I was thinking only of reaching the Chevalier's chateau by nightfall when by the strangest of fates–I saw her again–on my path.

KERMADEC: The one you love?

SIR WILLIAMS: Yes, Madame. So, I urged my horse across the fields and the woods, not listening to any other sounds but the violent pulsations of my heart. My horse led me to your door.

KERMADEC: This person then, is already married?

SIR WILLIAMS: No–her hand is free.

KERMADEC: Is it you who–

SIR WILLIAMS: Alas! I am without family. I'm 30 years old and have 200,000 pounds.

KERMADEC: Then you could marry her?

SIR WILLIAMS: Yes–if she loved me.

KERMADEC: And she doesn't love you?

SIR WILLIAMS: She loves someone else.

KERMADEC: What you're telling me is surprising. I don't see anyone in the neighborhood who–

SIR WILLIAMS: She was at the Saut-du-Moine with her mother.

KERMADEC: Ah! Her name is Hermine!

SIR WILLIAMS: You know her?

KERMADEC: She's my niece.

SIR WILLIAMS: Your–your niece?

KERMADEC: Yes, my niece! So she's the one who refuses to love you? Who does she love then?

SIR WILLIAMS: A man unworthy of her love.

KERMADEC: For goodness' sake, I would like to see that! She can't–as soon as she gets here, I will–

SIR WILLIAMS: She's coming here?

KERMADEC: I'm expecting her for supper.

SIR WILLIAMS: I can't bear to see her! Goodbye, Madame.

(*He leaves hurriedly. Jonas returns.*)

JONAS (*bewildered*): Madame! Madame! The knightly gentleman has got back on his horse and left. He races like the Devil, for sure!

KERMADEC: And worse, a Devil in love! There's still some romance left in this world, Jonas. Just like when I was 20! That was a fine time then!

(*She goes to the piano and strikes several keys.*)

KERMADEC: Then one never feared neither death–nor love. Ah! How I was able to laugh over my passions with a song. Do you still remember it? (*singing*)

> They say all desires
> Change with age,
> Little children love candy
> Later trumpets and drums

But at twenty the heart quakes
And you love without
Really loving anybody
I love Chiquito the Caballero
Oh! Oh! Oh!

<u>Refrain</u>
Ah! Chiquito! Chiquito! My king!
I don't know anyone
More handsome than you!
When I see you in the square
On your horse, or walking on foot
Ah! Chiquito! Chiquito! My king!
Come, I'm yours–
Do with me what you will,
Chiquito! My King!

(*Monsieur de Beaupréau, Thérèse and Hermine enter quietly and listen with some amazement to the Baronesse singing. Jonas has made himself scarce.*)

ALL: Bravo! Bravo! Auntie! We didn't know you had this talent.
THÉRÈSE: Auntie–You're just as young as ever.
KERMADEC: Plague take that man and his abrupt departure. He's got me all mixed up.
THÉRÈSE: Of what man are you speaking, Auntie?
KERMADEC: An Englishman who just left here. Sir Williams.
BEAUPRÉAU: Then it was him?
KERMADEC: He said he saw you at the Saut-du-Moine.
BEAUPRÉAU: More than that! He saved me from certain death.

KERMADEC: You were in danger?

BEAUPRÉAU: My runaway horse was going to throw me over the cliff when he managed to pull him back.

KERMADEC: As I suspected it; that man is a true knight!

BEAUPRÉAU: Where is he?

KERMADEC: When I told him Hermine was my niece, he ran away as if the Devil himself was after him.

THÉRÈSE: Without saying why?

BEAUPRÉAU: He's a sad character, an unhappy man who deserves our sympathy.

HERMINE: Then you know him, father?

BEAUPRÉAU: Why–so do you! He danced with you at the Ministry's ball.

HERMINE: Ah yes. He isn't bad.

KERMADEC: Do you know who Sir Williams is in love with, my pretty niece?

HERMINE: How would you expect me to know that?

BEAUPRÉAU: The impression you made on him at that ball was so powerful that he asked me for your hand. As you were already engaged at the time, I demurred but I am truly sorry to have done so.

KERMADEC: You will have to meet this Prince Charming, my niece. By all that's holy, you can't but fall in love with him. (*she takes her cue on the piano and starts singing again*)

> Ah! Chiquito! Chiquito! My king!
> I don't know anyone
> More handsome than you!
> When I see you in the square
> On your horse, or walking on foot
> Ah! Chiquito! Chiquito! My king!
> Come, I'm yours–

Do with me what you will,
Chiquito! My King!

CURTAIN

ACT IV

Scene XVII

The cellar at The Rendezvous des Quatre Hussars. There is an impressive collection of wine casks. Spider webs hang from the ceiling. Some pots, various bits of crockery and empty bottles litter the floor. A narrow stairway of stone steps descending from the floor above is the only access.

SIR WILLIAMS (*walking down the stairs preceded by Rocambole, a candle in hand*): Listen to me, lad–I want to know what happened here. Where is Colar?

ROCAMBOLE: I understand, Boss. But what I have to tell you can't be done in full daylight. We barely escaped and the birds almost flew off.

SIR WILLIAMS: What? Jeanne and Cerise?

ROCAMBOLE: But I'm a resourceful customer. Even though he had me at the point of his gun, I lured him to the banks of the Seine and, there, I properly dispatched him into the river. As he kept clinging to me, we both took a cold bath and–

SIR WILLIAMS: Enough of your incessant prattle. For the last time, where is Colar?

ROCAMBOLE: Right before you, Boss.

SIR WILLIAMS: If he was, I would see him. This cellar isn't so large.

ROCAMBOLE: No, it isn't but a cask is smaller yet; and friend Colar can keep in a cask.

SIR WILLIAMS: Stop joking, Rocambole.

ROCAMBOLE: A cask is, after all, not unlike a casket, and there's nothing funny about either. Especially when we're talking about Colar's latest abode.

SIR WILLIAMS: What are you talking about?

ROCAMBOLE: Colar is dead, Boss, but we haven't had time to bury him yet.

SIR WILLIAMS: Dead!

ROCAMBOLE: Yes, Boss. Right inside that cask.

(*He goes tapping the barrels until one gives off a different sound from the others, then he turns it over and Colar's body appears, curled up but otherwise perfectly preserved.*)

SIR WILLIAMS: By Jove! It's indeed Colar and his eyes will never again see the light of day. But where and how was he killed?

ROCAMBOLE: Upstairs, about 12 days ago, by a bullet through his chest.

SIR WILLIAMS: Ah? He died from a pistol shot?

ROCAMBOLE: Yes, Boss. The Comte killed him–The Comte de Kergaz.

SIR WILLIAMS: Armand? Why, this means he's hot on Jeanne's trail!

ROCAMBOLE: And Cerise's. That's the story I was trying to tell you but you kept shushing me.

SIR WILLIAMS: Good old Colar! He was a loyal and dedicated man; it'll be hard to replace him.

ROCAMBOLE: Yes, he was a brave sort. But now that I know the job–I'll be happy to take over under the same terms.

SIR WILLIAMS: You, replacing Colar? I don't think so. I wanted to ask him to confess to the theft of 30,000 francs–of which Fernand Rocher is innocent–and who I now would be unhappy to see condemned. I have my reasons for that.

ROCAMBOLE: I understand. In that case, naturally, I prefer that you find somebody else for the job.

SIR WILLIAMS: Still, Colar, wouldn't have turned me down...

ROCAMBOLE: Then it's really a shame he's dead.

SIR WILLIAMS: We need to sort this out. What about Nicolo? He was present at the murder. You must know where he lives.

ROCAMBOLE: Yes, in a hovel in Paris.

SIR WILLIAMS: What would Maman Fipart say?

ROCAMBOLE: If there was something in it for her, she'd be happy to sell him to the Devil.

SIR WILLIAMS: And you–what terms are you on with him?

ROCAMBOLE: Truthfully, I find him irritating. I'd be happy to see him guillotined.

SIR WILLIAMS: If my memory serves me correctly, Nicolo has a checkered past (*consulting his notebook*) Twenty years in the galleys for theft and murder–an escape from Rochefort–for the Police. a man like him is perfectly capable of murder, and since we must *pay the Law*–he'll be it. He'll be the one who murdered Colar.

ROCAMBOLE: Even though it was the Comte de Kergaz?

SIR WILLIAMS: Even though.

ROCAMBOLE: You do realize that after he's arrested, he'll deny it.

SIR WILLIAMS: We'll have witnesses.

ROCAMBOLE: Who?

SIR WILLIAMS: Well, first of all–you, my lad! You'll swear under oath that you saw Nicolo shoot Colar.

ROCAMBOLE: Any other witnesses?

SIR WILLIAMS: Yes. Maman Fipart! Let's ask her. She must still be upstairs?

ROCAMBOLE: Yes, Boss. Even she must be wondering what nefarious schemes are being concocted in her cellar.

SIR WILLIAMS: Well, go and reassure her as to the fate of her wine bottles and ask her to come down.

ROCAMBOLE: Right, Boss.

(*He clambers up the stairs four at a time.*)

SIR WILLIAMS (*addressing Colar's body*): A few words if I may, old friend. Here's a note that I wanted you to carry. Now that you're dead, you're even less likely to refuse. Coquelet wrote it in a style that imitates your handwriting–he's a master at his craft, that one–and it's addressed to our friends in London. In it, you admit to the theft at the Ministry and you promise to pay the *Gentlemen of the Night* what you owe them with the proceeds of this latest robbery. I'll take your billfold in exchange for this letter–also two or three compromising letters you kept. And your purse and your watch for which you no longer have a use. There, now we're quits. Thank you for everything and may the Devil be kind to you. (*he turns over the barrel*)

(*Rocambole returns with Maman Fipart.*)

MAMAN FIPART (*grumbling*): What an idea to make me come down to the cellar with my old leg.

SIR WILLIAMS: We have serious matters to discuss, woman. You are aware that Nicolo killed Colar.

MAMAN FIPART: What? Nicolo didn't kill Colar–

SIR WILLIAMS: Your eyes betray you again, Maman Fipart. Remember–Nicolo killed Colar. Rocambole saw him–didn't you, Rocambole?

ROCAMBOLE: With my own two eyes. Clear as daylight, Boss.

MAMAN FIPART (*understanding*): Ah yes! Of course, Nicolo killed Colar. What was I thinking! That wretched man has pissed me off for a long time. Let him go to prison for a bit; it'll do him some good.

SIR WILLIAMS: So you will say so to the Police?

MAMAN FIPART: I don't like ratting someone to the Law–even Nicolo.

SIR WILLIAMS: You must do it–you will do it. You'll tell them remorse compelled you to tell the truth.

MAMAN FIPART: What truth?

SIR WILLIAMS: The whole truth. Our truth. Rocambole will go with you. Here's what you will tell them. The night of the crime, Nicolo and Colar came here for a drink. They talked for a while, speaking in whispers. Colar was going to leave France after stealing the money from the Ministry, but a quarrel arose about dividing up the loot, Nicolo got mad and shot him dead. After having stolen Colar's purse and watch, Nicolo swore you to silence and forced you to hide the body in your cellar.

ROCAMBOLE: How much will mama get for her testimony?

SIR WILLIAMS: Three hundred francs.

ROCAMBOLE: That's not much. Nicolo risks his head in the bargain. It'll be bad for business. That's worth at least 1,000 francs.

SIR WILLIAMS: Go for 1,000 francs.

ROCAMBOLE: And 500 francs for me for supervising the job.

SIR WILLIAMS: Yes, if you hide this purse and this watch inside Nicolo's mattress.

ROCAMBOLE: Of course! The Police will never hear more truthful and moving testimony–I swear it with my hand in the air.

CURTAIN

The edge of a forest in Brittany. The old Chevalier de Lacy is waiting in full hunting gear as Sir Williams arrives.

LACY: You're in the nick of time, my dear Sir Williams! I'm leaving for the hunt and I'll be delighted to take you along.

SIR WILLIAMS: Gladly! I've just returned from Paris and I feel myself wishing terribly to kill a ten-horn or some old buck.

LACY: You mustn't have succeeded in your plans.

SIR WILLIAMS: Indeed! I'm at the end of my rope!

LACY: In two words, put me in the picture. You have saved that young man with whom Mademoiselle Hermine was taken?

SIR WILLIAMS: Completely.

LACY: Then he wasn't guilty?

SIR WILLIAMS: On the contrary.

LACY: You've earned a fine title to her gratitude that way. How did you do it?

SIR WILLIAMS: I merely offered a reward. It was necessary to find a man who would consent to admitting he was the author of the theft–a large enough reward–

LACY: Very ingenious–and you found such a man?

SIR WILLIAMS: By means of 100,000 francs, yes. But it didn't bring him luck.

LACY: How's that?

SIR WILLIAMS: The man I found was named Colar. He was an escaped convict. My proposition made him leap with joy, but his newfound fortune was soon lost. A greedy tavern-keeper who'd discovered his secret murdered him to steal the money.

LACY: Is the Police–

SIR WILLIAMS: Yes, The Police have already got involved and the thief was arrested.

LACY: In that case, there's only one thing left for you to do.

SIR WILLIAMS: Which is?

LACY: Inform Mademoiselle de Beaupréau of your actions.

SIR WILLIAMS: That's exactly what I was proposing to do.

LACY: And all that remains for her is to keep her promise.

SIR WILLIAMS (*pretending astonishment*): What promise?

LACY: That she would marry you if you'd save the young man from dishonor.

SIR WILLIAMS: I don't intend to remind her of it.

LACY: You would renounce?

SIR WILLIAMS: Not at all. But I understand the psychology of women. Hermine made that promise in a moment of exaltation. It would be not generous of me to take advantage–

LACY: Come on! A promise is a promise.

SIR WILLIAMS: I don't wish to force her hand.

CURTAIN

Scene XIX

A small room in the Chateau of the Baronesse Kermadec. Same setting as Scene IV, Act III.

HERMINE (*dressed as a bride*): Yes, Sir Williams, the delicacy of your feelings has deeply touched me. The urgency that brought you here to tell me the happy news, while releasing me from my promise was the act of a true, gallant man.

SIR WILLIAMS: Only the love that I feel for you dictated my conduct. I'm convinced that anyone else in my place–

HERMINE: Don't diminish your merit. Let the affection and gratitude that I will have for you all my life make you forget the love that you would have had the right to expect from the woman who will bear your name–

SIR WILLIAMS: That's more than I dared to hope for!

(*Enter the Baronesse de Kermadec and the Chevalier de Lacy, both dressed in ceremonial Empire style.*)

KERMADEC: Look at our lovers, Chevalier, look at them. They're adorable! When I think that, without you, the Baronet would be in London and my delightful little niece would still be pursuing her childish dream... (*to Hermine*) How much more beautiful is the reality, isn't that so, darling?

HERMINE: You're the best of aunts

KERMADEC: The best? Why, you don't have any others! (*to Lacy*) Eighty years old and no one here to help me. I have to watch over everything. The guests are already arriving. And the Notary hasn't arrived yet!

LACY: Would you like me to go and look for him, Madame?

KERMADEC: Would you, Chevalier? You're amiability itself. To reward you, I'll dance the first waltz with you.

LACY: I accept, Madame! I accept!

(*He leaves laughing.*)

KERMADEC (*going closer to Hermine and Williams*): Since we're alone, my children, allow me to give you some advice which will enrich your life. Have for each other the amorous eyes of Chiquito–that of my song. (*her fingers leaf over the piano and she hums the refrain*) That's the secret of happiness.

(*Lacy returns with Monsieur de Beaupréau, Thérèse and a man who is obviously the Notary.*)

LACY (*smiling*): I've found the Notary, my beautiful friend.

KERMADEC (*to Notary*): Monsieur, please read us the contract you have prepared.

(*Everyone sits around the Notary. He puts on his reading glasses, coughs, then unfolds a voluminous notebook and begins reading in a monotonous tone.*)

NOTARY: Before Monsieur de Coz, Notary at Kerloven, the undersigned have appeared...

(*But their attention is suddenly distracted by the appearance of a new arrival, dressed in dirty and dusty traveling clothes.*)

JONAS (*announcing*): Monsieur le Comte Armand de Kergaz.

(*Everyone rises, surprised.*)

COMTE DE KERGAZ (*bowing to the Baronesse*): Please, Madame, forgive me for daring to appear before you in such an outfit. Believe me, indeed, when I say that, to dare disturb the noblest and most beautiful of all family gatherings, I had to have the most compelling of reasons, and only an imperious necessity made me–
KERMADEC: I believe you, Monsieur. Speak.
COMTE DE KERGAZ: I am the Executor of the will of the late Baron Kermor de Kermarouet, a Breton gentleman whose fortune was estimated to be in the neighborhood of 12 millions francs –isn't that so, Sir Williams?
SIR WILLIAMS (*pretending ignorance*): What? I'm afraid, Monsieur, I know not this Baron you speak of, nor–
COMTE DE KERGAZ: No matter. I will explain. (*to the Baronesse*) But first, may I ask you, Madame, to entreat the Notary to leave us alone for a moment?
KERMADEC (*to Lacy*): Damn this Comte de Kergaz and his delays. But he speaks with so much authority–

(*At a gesture from the Baronesse, the Notary withdraws. Monsieur de Beaupréau edges closer to Sir Williams. Meanwhile, the Comte de Kergaz walks towards Hélène de Beaupréau.*)

COMTE DE KERGAZ: Madame, do you recognize this medallion?
THÉRÈSE: Yes–I–who stole it from me?

COMTE DE KERGAZ: A man whom God has already cruelly punished–and who, in his last hour, directed me to beg for your forgiveness–yours and that of your child's–his child's.

SIR WILLIAMS (*aside to Beaupréau*): Our business has taken a turn for the worse, father-in-law. Stay by my side, be ready for any eventuality–

HERMINE (*throwing herself into Thérèse's arms*): Mama! What does this man mean?

COMTE DE KERGAZ (*solemnly*): The Baron Kermor de Kermarouet designated his natural child, Mademoiselle Hermine de Beaupréau, as his sole heir. You will agree, Ladies and Gentlemen, that under these conditions, the proposed marriage contract between Mademoiselle de Beaupréau and Sir Williams ought to be withdrawn. Had I arrived only an hour later, and Sir Williams had become the spouse of Mademoiselle de Beaupréau, he would have been 12 millions richer.

SIR WILLIAMS (*raising his head*): Monsieur, I swear most solemnly that until you spoke, I was entirely unaware that Mademoiselle de Beaupréau had any dowry; and further that I am myself rich enough for her and for me.

COMTE DE KERGAZ: Really? My inquiries have, on the contrary, revealed that one of London's most notorious criminals was recently run out of that city by his fellow thieves and came to Paris to seek his fortune. Having learned of the will of the late Baron de Kermarouet, this man then wove a vast criminal conspiracy, which I have begun to unravel today.

SIR WILLIAMS: These slanderous accusations have one major defect: they are without proof.

COMTE DE KERGAZ: You want proof–you shall have it!

(*He leaves in a general silence and returns swiftly with Fernand and Baccarat. At the sight of her former fiancé, Hermine falls into Thérèse's arms.*)

COMTE DE KERGAZ: Monsieur de Beaupréau–is this your employee, Fernand Rocher? Sir Williams, do you recognize this woman known throughout Paris as La Baccarat and whom you had recently committed against her will to a lunatic asylum?

(*Beaupréau and Sir Williams are unable to repress a shiver.*)

FERNAND (*to Beaupréau*): Monsieur, before your family gathered here, I appeal to your honor. You know better than anyone how the 30,000 francs were stolen from the Ministry. I demand that you proclaim publicly that they were never, even for a moment, in my hands and that I am not a thief.

(*Beaupréau lowers his head without replying.*)

BACCARAT (*on her knees to Hermine*): Mademoiselle, I've been unworthy and I'm here to try to repair the evil I've done. I loved the one you had chosen to be your spouse with a mad passion. I became caught in the evil web of lies spun by Sir Williams. I have suffered in my flesh and in my heart more than I have ever suffered in my whole life. But I knew where my duty lie and I went to the Police–
HERMINE (*with a scream of liberation*): Then, it's not Sir Williams who saved Fernand? It's you! Fernand! I've got you back–free and innocent!

COMTE DE KERGAZ (*to Sir Williams*): Your evil edifice of lies is collapsing. Do you hear me, Andrea? Yes, I know that, too! (*pointing to the door*) Get out!

THÉRÈSE (*to Beaupréau*): I hope, Monsieur, that you won't have the audacity to want to be present at the marriage of my daughter with the honest man you sought to dishonor. I ask you to leave!

SIR WILLIAMS (*with effrontery*): It seems you win again, brother, but still, my hour will come. (*to Beaupréau*) Come, "father-in-law." We're beaten but we will still have our revenge.

(*Sir Williams and Beaupréau leave.*)

COMTE DE KERGAZ (to *Hermine and Fernand who are embracing each other*): You are worthy of each other. Be happy! (*to Baccarat*) And you who were once La Baccarat, lean on my arm and remember that God forgives those who have suffered greatly.

KERMADEC (*at the window*): Oh! Chevalier, look! The Baronet and my nephew have leaped into the Comte's coach and kicked its coachman out! They're riding out! It's just like a romance novel!

COMTE DE KERGAZ: The bandits! Quick! Let me have a horse.

(*He leaves precipitously.*)

KERMADEC: Jonas! Jonas! Give our new friend that horse there! (*to Lacy*) Excuse me, Chevalier, I seem to have loaned your horse to the Comte de Kergaz. Until its return, you will of course remain my guest.

CURTAIN

Scene XX

The garden of the villa de Bougival at night. Same décor as in Act II, Scene I. Maman Fipart is seated at a table, reading a book by the light of a lantern.

ROCAMBOLE (*entering*): Mama? You're still up at this hour?

MAMAN FIPART: My son, we shouldn't have denounced Nicolo. I feel some remorse and it prevents me from sleeping.

ROCAMBOLE: Ah, Mama, you still have a way of getting a laugh.

MAMAN FIPART: Look out! Here's company. (*places her book down*)

(*Sir Williams and Beaupréau enter, each with a lantern in hand.*)

SIR WILLIAMS (*to Beaupréau*): Good! Maman Fipart and Rocambole are still up–that will help.

BEAUPRÉAU: Six horses left dead of fatigue on the road. We couldn't have made it any faster if the Devil himself had been at our heels. I can't take any more.

SIR WILLIAMS: This is fun, "father-in-law"! Be assured that that damnable Comte de Kergaz is already on our tracks. He must make it fast.

MAMAN FIPART: Sir Williams–

SIR WILLIAMS: Tonight, for the purpose of my little charade, call me Comte de Kergaz.

ROCAMBOLE: I see that you brought with you an old acquaintance, Boss–Monsieur de Beaupréau.

SIR WILLIAMS: You must be mistaken lad. Tonight, this gentleman is Léon Rolland.

ROCAMBOLE (*without being duped*): Yes, of course. I must have lost my head–

SIR WILLIAMS: Go fetch Cerise and tell her that her lover is waiting for her.

ROCAMBOLE (*expecting the order, amused*): Right, Boss.

(*Exit Rocambole.*)

SIR WILLIAMS (*to Maman Fipart*): While they gossip, I'll talk to Jeanne. Go–wake her very gently. I have notions of strolling in moonlight while declaiming poetry.

(*Maman Fipart leaves.*)

SIR WILLIAMS (*to Beaupréau*): Well, "father-in-law," my 12 millions are gone, Hermine is already likely married to another, but all the same, I pay my debts. Tonight, Cerise is yours.

BEAUPRÉAU: What you are doing–it's–monstrous.

SIR WILLIAMS: Ah, "father-in-law!" Don't go acting noble on me. Don't forget we're here to get revenge!

(*He takes the lantern and disappears into the night.*)

MAMAN FIPART (*off stage*): This way, Mademoiselle Cerise, this way. There's a nice surprise for you.

(Cerise enters and steps into the light of the lantern Beaupréau had placed on the table. Beaupréau remains in the shadows.)

CERISE: Léon? Where are you?
BEAUPRÉAU *(still in the shadows)*: I'm here!
CERISE: Your voice has changed–

(Beaupréau jumps out of the shadows and grabs Cerise in his arms.)

CERISE: You're not Léon!
BEAUPRÉAU: Cerise, my beautiful Cerise, I adore you!
CERISE *(struggling)*: No! Let me go!
BEAUPRÉAU: Don't you recognize me? I'm your friend–the one who wishes you well!
CERISE *(struggling)*: Help! Léon!
BEAUPRÉAU: Léon is far away and no one can hear you.
CERISE: Rocambole! Rocambole! Sir Williams!

(Sir Williams returns with Maman Fipart.)

SIR WILLIAMS *(to Beaupréau)*: Get back, knave! *(to Cerise)*: What do you want, pretty one?
CERISE: I want to die!
SIR WILLIAMS: You know that I am a doctor. Take this cordial. *(offers her a drink which she swallows rapidly)*
CERISE: I have confidence in you. I feel better, thanks
SIR WILLIAMS: Hola! Madame Fipart, take Mademoiselle Cerise to her room.

(Maman Fipart and Cerise leave.)

SIR WILLIAMS (*to Beaupréau*): I've given her a drug that will make her pliant to your will. I abandon her to your tender mercies.

BEAUPRÉAU: Thank you.

(*Beaupréau leaves.*)

SIR WILLIAMS (*alone*): And now, Jeanne–the two of us.

(*Jeanne enters, escorted by Rocambole; she is in an elegant déshabillé. Half-awake, she heads toward the light of the lantern. Sir Williams remains in the shadows.*)

ROCAMBOLE: The Comte Armand de Kergaz–

(*He swiftly eclipses himself.*)

SIR WILLIAMS: Jeanne, my darling Jeanne.

JEANNE: The veils of night are enveloping this garden so deeply that I'm unable to discover the one who calls me and whom my heart desires? Is that you, Armand?

SIR WILLIAMS (*emerging from the shadows*): At last I find you again. Jeanne my beloved–Jeanne my sole and only love.

JEANNE: Who are you, Monsieur?

SIR WILLIAMS: The one who awaits you. The one whose inflamed letters you've deigned to read.

JEANNE: You're Armand?

SIR WILLIAMS: Yes, I'm the Comte de Kergaz.

JEANNE: Then what Cerise told me is really true? Why did you call yourself Sir Williams then?

SIR WILLIAMS: All that seems strange to you is going to be explained. Yes, I am the Comte Armand de Kergaz, master of an immense fortune In my youth, I had to choose: either to waste it stupidly, like many sons of good families–or to spend it nobly doing good. I have chosen the latter, but what I had to do to achieve my goal has forced me to change my name. As I continued my studies in England, I became the Baronet Sir Williams. Then, one day, I learned that you were going to fall into an infamous trap. I knew your pains, your isolation, your beauty, your virtue. I saw you and I loved you.

JEANNE: You speak of danger, of a trap?

SIR WILLIAMS: Yes. Last Sunday, didn't you go to Belleville in company of Cerise and her fiancé?

JEANNE: Please continue.

SIR WILLIAMS: There, two men showed up and sought a quarrel with Léon Rolland.

JEANNE: Indeed.

WILLIAMS: Then, a third man drove off the two villains and you invited him to join you–along with young Rocambole, who you saw again here later.

JEANNE: All this's true, Monsieur.

SIR WILLIAMS: That third man was dressed like a worker; he gave you his arm and escorted you inside, right? (*Jeanne gestures in acquiescence*) But the next day, another man, an old man dressed like a soldier, came to reside in your house, on the same floor as you. He claimed he was a Captain, called himself Bastien and pretended to have been a friend of your father? (*another nod from Jeanne*) Then the other man who had escorted you showed up and used my name and my title and you believed him. Well, that man was playing an odious game. In Belleville, with the so-called Captain Bastien and with you. That man lied.

JEANNE: It's impossible.

SIR WILLIAMS: I ought to have warned you of the danger. But you were on the point of falling in love with this man. To save you, I had no choice but to have you carried away and taken here during your sleep. But then, I didn't dare show myself, so I wrote to you. And I almost died with joy when I received your first reply.

JEANNE: But, Monsieur, if you are the true Comte de Kergaz, then who is the man who's assumed your name?

SIR WILLIAMS: My former servant. That wretch has used my name to dupe you.

JEANNE (*stunned*): That man was–how could I have been deceived to that degree?

SIR WILLIAMS: Forget what has already happened. A future of happiness awaits you. Jeanne, my adored, I love you and you're going to love me. Your noble mind has already seen the difference between the real and the false Comte de Kergaz. Already, a strange and powerful harmony brings us together. Let me gather from your lips– (*he entwines her and leans down to kiss her*)

JEANNE (*quickly disengaging herself from the embrace*): No! No! I don't love you. You can't be the Comte de Kergaz. A real gentleman doesn't behave as you've just done.

SIR WILLIAMS (*enraged*): So be it then! You're right, I'm not the Comte de Kergaz. My name's Andrea de Felipone, Andrea the disinherited, Andrea the cursed! Andrea, the brother of the one whom you love and whom I hate! I hate him the way Hell hates Heaven! And you, you're going to love me despite yourself. I will have you!

(*Jeanne defends herself. Sir Williams subdues her violently and applies a kiss forcefully to her lips.*)

SIR WILLIAMS: I love you with a passion so fierce that–you'll belong to me despite Armand–who is far from here, who's already forgotten you–

(*Suddenly, he recoils; Jeanne has just plunged a dagger into his heart.*)

SIR WILLIAMS: Ah–

(*The Comte de Kergaz enters, pistol in hand.*)

COMTE DE KERGAZ: Andrea! The hour of punishment has come!
JEANNE (*haggard*): Hear me, O God–didn't I have the right to defend myself?
SIR WILLIAMS: You're too late, hated brother. I'm dying. (*collapses*)
COMTE DE KERGAZ (*leaning over Sir Williams*): May God be your judge. (*closes his brother's eyes.*)

(*After having crossed himself, he stands up. Jeanne, still terrified, nestles herself into his arms.*)

JEANNE: At last, I find you, Armand. If you knew how I suffered in your absence.

(*Rocambole enters.*)

ROCAMBOLE: Monsieur le Comte, I am pleased to put myself at your service. Do you remember the day I escorted you to the home of the Baron de Kermarouet?

COMTE DE KERGAZ: Silence, lad. My brother has just died.

ROCAMBOLE: You should have recognized in his eyes the same flame that you saw in the eyes of Doctor Johnson.

COMTE DE KERGAZ: You mean–the doctor who miraculously allowed the Baron to express his last wishes?

ROCAMBOLE: Yes. The doctor in whom you said you recognized the hand of God.

COMTE DE KERGAZ: Ah, what a strange creature that man was! At least, let the lesson profit you, Rocambole, and know that, sooner or later, he who does ill, always expiates his sins.

CURTAIN

www.ingramcontent.com/pod-product-compliance
Lightning Source LLC
Chambersburg PA
CBHW060351030726
47497CB00003B/678